Helga

'Tears of blood.'

By

Kevin Heads

I dedicate this book to my wife

Susan Patricia Heads

And my daughter

Stephanie May Heads

Some Warriors fight for glory

Real Warriors fight to survive

Chapter One

My mother told me that the Goddess shaped the world. She crafted the mountains, the sea, and all the lands that sat upon it. She forged the animals in her giant fire and placed them where she felt they would best thrive. Then she gathered stars from the night sky and crushed them into a fine powder, mixing them gently with soil and water from a clear mountain stream. From that paste, she moulded people, and we made her smile. She was so pleased with us that with her breath she gave life to her creation, and blessed us with the greatest gift of all, the ability to love.

Yet on that day, I saw no love, just cruelty and butchery. An event of barbarism that would haunt my dreams and remain embedded in my heart forever.

∞

I sat quietly whilst my mother added another log to the blazing fire. The yellow and orange sparks jumped and skipped along the stone-built walls of our simple dwelling. I listened intently whilst my mother regaled stories of long ago and far-off places. A time when our tribes joined forces and fought glorious battles against the legions of Rome. I was a Pict and proud of my heritage.

Weariness laid its hands upon my shoulders; after spending much of my day foraging around the nearby standing stones; searching out mushrooms, berries and wild herbs for food and healing. I now sat quietly, trying desperately to stay awake.

I was ten summers old and every day for me was magical and wondrous. Surrounded by the northern sea, we lived a simple island life, and were at the mercy of the Goddess and the elements for all our provisions. Luckily for us, this year's harvest had been plentiful, and it was a time of glorious celebration. Our goddess had been more than kind, and we were all thankful.

My eyes were so heavy, and I could feel myself drifting off into the land of dreams, when my father entered our home and placed a freshly caught Hake over the spitting fire. It sizzled and spat and I watched, mesmerized, as its eyes melted within the golden flames. He removed his hooded cloak and warmed himself. The autumn chill had entered with him and it made me shiver, jolting me back from the edge of sleep.

'We will not go hungry this winter.' My father smiled, patting me on the head. 'Our crops have flourished and we will start harvesting in the morning.'

'I will make an offering to give thanks,' my mother nodded. 'Eithne can help me.'

'I can?'

I was so surprised, as my mother had only ever done this alone.

'You can. I will teach you.' My mother grinned at me and

laughed when I hugged her tight. My father reached out and tugged at my red locks, making me squeal as he pulled me in close. I laugh uncontrollably as his powerful hands tickled me roughly.

'Where's my hug?' he demanded.

I leapt onto him excitedly, encircling his broad neck with my skinny little arms. He held me close, enjoying the moment, reluctant to let me loose.

'Mother?' I asked as I wriggled from my father's grip and lay across his lap, snuggling into his shoulder and chest.

'What is it, child?' she replied, turning the fish over in the spitting flames.

'Is our Goddess more powerful than the one God?'

There was a moment's silence before she answered.

'There are many gods and goddesses in our world Eithne, some have unfamiliar names, yet many are the same. This one God you are referring to, however, seems to me to be a God of punishment and cruelty, a male God who lives in the heavens and wants to dominate all those upon the land and sea. He rules by fear, not love, and many will die under the shadow of his cross, I fear.'

I was frightened of this God. I had heard rumours from the mainland that his power had spread throughout our people, and that grand churches were being built in his name. Many had already converted to his ways, and his hand was creeping ever closer to my home.

'We should not talk about this one God in fear of angering our own,' my father added sternly. 'Now let's eat and talk about other things.'

I noticed my father's unease as I climbed from his knee. We had heard that on one of the smaller islands, priests had arrived and were building a small place of worship to their God. They were teaching his ways, preaching that he was the only veritable god and that all other gods were false idols. I did not believe this, but some in our village feared this god and wondered if he was more powerful than our own.

A few from our village had visited this place, making the journey when the sea was calm enough to sail. They had all returned with small wooden crosses, a gift from God, the priests had told them. This made my father so angry, he too believed that this God was the God of greed and war and to worship such a God would only bring death, destruction and misfortune to us all.

There was an awkward silence, and I wished I had not mentioned it, but I felt the more I knew of such things, the better prepared I would be should this God come to my island.

My father removed the fish from the flames and added another. The smell was so divine and I was pleased that he offered me the first bite. I was so hungry.

'Eat, for tomorrow is a big day for you. Our Goddess will be watching you closely, daughter.'

He emphasized the word 'our' and it didn't go unnoticed by my mother or me. I felt somewhat embarrassed, but I was young and inquisitive and wanted to learn about all the things in my world, the good and the bad.

That night I barely slept; I was so excited at the prospect of helping my mother prepare the offering. The first day of harvest was a big occasion for our village. At sunset, we would sacrifice a pig, roast it above a blazing fire and a sumptuous feast would begin; but not until my mother had made the offering. She was our priestess, as her mother had been before her. It was a great honour and brought high status to our family. I hoped one day that I too would follow in her footsteps and perform the rites and rituals for my people, and today would mark the beginning of that journey.

I was up bright and early, yawning at the rising sun as it peeked over the crashing waves. Its low light cast a golden glow across the rolling landscape and beaches of my island home.

The wind was strong as I made my way along the sprawling sands, eagerly searching among the rocks and pools for crabs and mussels. Colourful shells that their inhabitants had long abandoned, and strands of seaweed and driftwood that I would use for decoration. I was careful to pick only the best pieces and smiled to myself as I placed my wares into my small wicker basket.

Skipping across the rocks and sand, I continued my search for anything that would make my goddess smile. This would be an offering like no other, I thought.

But if there is one thing I have learnt since that day, it is that the Gods can be fickle and cruel. Instead of being grateful for my efforts, she punished me and I didn't know why. Maybe I had angered her for speaking about the one God as my father had warned. I have pondered that thought many times since and blame myself for everything that happened on that fateful day. My life was about to be turned upside down and my idyllic island lifestyle shattered, destroyed, and lost forever.

The wind suddenly changed direction, rolling in from the east. It made the sea angry and agitated as it lifted foam from the choppy surface and flung it gently onto the rocks. It coated the sand and gathered in the pools, making it impossible for me to see the creatures that lay hidden beneath. Another gust playfully flicked a strand of my red hair across my eyes and I annoyingly stroked it away from my face. I cursed myself for not tying it back, as mother had suggested earlier that morning.

A flock of gulls started screaming excitedly further along the shoreline. I looked up but all I could see were mere dots in the now cloud filled sky. Their voices were shrill and foreboding, as if warning me of approaching danger. I ran towards them out of curiosity, but soon stopped when I noticed the black shape that rose from the deep.

There are no words to describe my panic and fear when I noticed the creature gliding through the bubbling surf. Its long neck pierced the waves and the sail on its back was a deep blood red. A white coiled serpent, ready to strike, lay upon the rippling fabric. The tide was incoming and with it came death.

I remember thinking, as I ran, that I was going to die. I had seen the shields and spears and heard the strange voices shouting from the monster's back. Their words were menacing and carried by the wistful wind. I raced through the dunes, my feet-sinking ankle deep, as if the monster had control of the sands beneath my feet and was trying to suck me down, making my escape slow and arduous. I turned in panic and saw men jumping down from the ship with shields now on their arms. Some carried spears, but most had swords or axes; they looked terrifying as they gathered together like a pack of wolves before the hunt.

I dropped my basket and used my hands to drag myself through the clinging sand. My feet kept slipping, sliding me back towards the invaded shore. I dropped to my knees and crawled frantically on all fours, grasping clumps of grass for leverage. I turned once more but could no longer see the men, only the serpent lurching back and forth with the gentle tide, its face glaring at me, mocking me. Suddenly and without warning, arms encircled my waist, and I was forcibly dragged across the dunes. Shocked and fearful, I screamed out.

'You're all right, Eithne, it's me.' I looked up and saw my father's face, which made me cry instantly. My tears flowed, dampening the dry sand beneath us as he hauled me into his arms and carried me to firmer ground. 'You must hide, run to the stones, don't go back to the village. Stay there and I will fetch you when it's safe.'

'Who are they?' I asked, still sobbing.

'They're Northmen, but these are not the usual traders; go now, don't let them catch you.' He kissed my head, then pushed me away. 'Run Eithne.'

My heart was pounding as I ran from the beach. I scurried

across the tall grasslands and through fields not yet harvested. Several sheep scattered as I approached and bleated pathetically, as if sensing my fear. The stones seemed so far away, but with each desperate stride, I knew they were getting nearer. My legs ached and my lungs burned with the exertion, so I was relieved as I neared the tall trees that surrounded the circle of standing stones. Trees were scant on my island; we cut most of them down many years ago for shelter and to make way for farming. This wood was not large, but it was big enough for a young girl to hide in.

The grass was still wet from the morning dew, the sun not yet reaching the dark recesses that I now entered, and in my haste, I slipped and gasped as I grazed against one of the large stones. My arm hurt like hell and I noticed blood oozing from a deep cut just below the elbow. Using my small knife that I always carried; I cut a piece of my tunic and tied it around the bloody wound.

Hidden from view, I stared at the standing stones. They had been here for hundreds of years, maybe a thousand. Many feared them, but not I. Some in our village had spoken of seeing creeping shadows within the circle and figures dancing in between the towering pillars. I didn't believe all the mysticism, but I sensed a power that was unexplainable. I loved being here, even at night, and I could almost hear our ancestors singing and praising the goddess for all the gifts she had given them. It was a wondrous place, but for now it was my sanctuary and I preyed in silence, hoping that Brigid, my goddess, would hear me.

I asked for protection and begged that the Northmen would leave us alone. I knew my father and the other men of the village would fight and try to protect our village, but they were few and the Northmen were many..

I listened intently, hoping for a sign, but the Goddess was silent, as if she too was in hiding. I wanted to move, to venture out across the treeless ground to see what was happening. It seemed so quiet, so peaceful. Even the birds had fallen silent.

Then I saw the smoke rising from the direction of my village. It was light at first, grey wisps flung sideways by the breath of the easterly wind. I watched as it turned darker and more menacing; it hung heavy in the salt-filled air and smeared the clear blue sky like a dirty stain. I knew then that my people were being slaughtered and our village destroyed. All I could do was stand and watch as day became night and the stars blossomed alongside the flickering flames that sparked into the night sky.

My father never came, and as the time passed, a deathly chill caressed my tired body and I fought the desperation to sleep. Once darkness came, I crept out of the trees and entered the stone circle for comfort. I sat with my back resting against one of the larger stones; it was warm to the touch, and I dozed lightly in its loving embrace.

I yearned for a deeper sleep, to be back in my home with a crackling fire for warmth and a belly filled with a satisfying stew. No food had passed my lips since that morning, and that very thought made my stomach growl and complain. I would need to find food when the daylight returned.

Just as I was finding a suitable place to lie down and rest, movement caught my eye. I froze, pulling my body inward, trying to be small, like a mouse.

They were shadows at first, but as they drew closer, I could see their shields and knew immediately that it was a few of the men from the serpent ship. I ducked behind the stone and lay flat on the ground as they approached. They were close, but did not enter the circle. I slipped into a small ditch that ran parallel to the stones; hugging the ground like a leveret hiding from an eagle. My heart thumped rapidly in my breast. It seemed so loud to me and I feared detection. Shaking away the irrational thought, I risked a peek above the edge of the ditch.

Men laughed, and I heard a woman scream. Scurrying silently along the narrow furrow, I reached the trees opposite to where the men now stood. Stepping back into the shadows, the darkness welcomed me in, rendering me invisible once more. I was about to retreat further when I heard the woman's voice; she was cursing at them in our native tongue, and I knew at once that it was my mother.

There is no good way to die, and my mother died brutally. I watched silently from the trees as the men took turns in raping her. One by one, they sodomized and abused her naked body. She fought hard at first; scratching, kicking and cursing, until exhausted by her own efforts she yielded, and let them pleasure themselves without resistance. After what seemed like an eternity, they tired of her and cast her aside like a broken spear; bored with her now battered body, they satisfied themselves by other means. A fire was lit, and they sat together laughing whilst drinking ale from their drinking horns.

If she had crawled away at that moment, she may have lived, but alas, she didn't. Instead, she raised herself up onto her hands and knees and crawled to the nearest stone. There, using its edges to pull herself to her feet, she swayed, hanging on tight as if the stones gave her power and strength. She was naked, and even under the moonlight, I could see the bruises on her battered body. I moved forward, thinking I could help, but stopped when one man stood and wobbled towards her. Although befuddled with ale, his purpose was obvious. My mother turned, hearing his approach. She smiled and invitingly spread her legs for him. Grabbing her throat, he pinned her to the stone with one hand, whilst removing his sword and pants with the other. His cock was flaccid, so my mother reached down and held it in her hand, stroking it gently. Moaning with pleasure, he released his grip on her throat. Then, whilst holding her head, he pushed her down the stone until her face was a few inches from his prick. Expecting the pleasure, he licked his lips, drool escaping from his bearded mouth. He sighed as my mother moved her head forward and took his now swollen member into her mouth. I gasped, but could not look away. He reached down with his hands and forced my mother's mouth deeper onto his shaft; she gagged then bit down hard. His screams echoed through the branches, and animals within earshot stampeded away. Staggering backward, he pushed my mother away as she spat out his disembodied phallus. The others started laughing, amused at their colleague's misfortune. That was until my mother, moving like a deer in flight, grabbed his sword, pulled it from its sheath, and thrust it forcefully into his ale-swollen belly. His eyes widened as he gasped and fell, my mother pulling the sword free as he hit the ground. Her nakedness was now adorned with his blood and her own. Droplets ran from her lips and across her breasts, and under the moon's gaze and in the shadows of the stones, she looked like a painted goddess coming to take their souls.

Staggering towards the others, determination etched upon her face, she screamed in anger. The men stood to greet her, but only one-stepped forward, and in one swift movement, his axe removed her head. I watched in silence as her executioner reached down and lifted it skyward, as if to show the goddess that he had taken her priestess and gained all her power. Nonchalantly, he threw it towards the others, his face smiling as he did so. The moon illuminated his face; he was tall, strong, with long black hair and an unkempt beard. His cheeks were painted with what looked like birds, one on each cheek, but I could not be certain in this light. It was a face I would never forget.

I was in despair and fell to my knees. Tears flowed like a waterfall of sorrow, and I was drowning in the deluge. I looked once more at my mother's dismembered body, cold and bloodless, a mere carcass, rich pickings for the crows and seabirds that would tear at her flesh in the morning light. It was then that I felt the anger rise; it started deep within my chest and then quickly crawled up my throat until I could taste its venom. Its poisonous loathing soured my mouth, but I savoured the flavour. Staggering to my feet, I took a step towards the band of men. I knew I would die or worse, but I didn't care. I had lost my mind. It now wandered the dark realms of grief and hate, so death would be a relief. One more step took me to the edge of the trees; I was numb and felt no fear. Another step and I would be out in the open and vulnerable. I removed my small knife from its sheath and made to step forward, but suddenly a hand covered my mouth, and pulled me back into the shadows. I looked up, hoping to see my father's face, but it was not to be; so I kicked and scratched, trying to break the powerful arms that held me so tight. I tried to wriggle free, but he just pulled me closer and whispered something incomprehensible into my ear. His language was like the others, but the dialect was different and in time I would learn to recognise the subtle differences. He whispered words that soothed my ire and calmed the rapids that tore a valley through my broken heart. His face was hidden, lost in the darkness by the hood that covered his head. However, I could still make out his long flowing hair; that seemed so fair, even within the pitchy blackness that engulfed us both.

He raised a finger to his lips, and I acknowledged the need for quiet. Slowly and hesitantly, he released his grip, believing I would flee, no doubt. I didn't. Instead, I just stood there silently, lost in my own thoughts, too traumatized and in shock from the horror of witnessing my mother's gory death. I shook; emotions overwhelming me as the memory played back over and over. He bent down and stroked my red locks and tear-stained cheeks, before picking me up once more and carrying me deeper into the woods where others emerged from the undergrowth to meet us. I counted eight, all well armed. Their shields were round like the others, but there was no serpent. I didn't know who they were, nor did I care. They quickly carried me away, through the trees and away from danger. I watched the stones getting smaller and smaller, the last attachment to my people and my former life. I sobbed uncontrollably and lay my head on my rescuers broad shoulder. As he nuzzled his face against mine, just like my father did, sleep descended, but there was no escaping the dreams that would now pursue me, dreams that still haunt to this day.

CHAPTER TWO

It was dawn when I awoke. The sun was hidden behind rain-filled clouds, dark and threatening. They stretched out lazily towards the distant horizon, their greyness mirrored by the rolling waves that cradled the ship that clung to the shoreline.

The tide was incoming, and they were preparing to leave. The ship was much smaller than the serpent ship, broader too. Shields hung along its sides, but I got the impression this was more a trading vessel than a fighting ship.

Someone nearby shouted, and although his language was foreign to me, I guessed what he had said, as everyone present turned and stared in my direction.

I was lying next to a dying fire. Its red glow and grey ash were all that remained. It was slight, but it gave some warmth against the autumnal chill. The beach was filled with men loading the ship. Provisions for the winter months, I guessed.

Jumping to my feet, I tried to run, but came to a jolted halt as an arm reached out and grabbed my waist, lifting me high into the air. I screamed and fought back, hammering my fists upon my abductors back. I spat and cussed, remembering my mother's cursing in moments of anger. That sudden memory hurt and made me kick and swear even harder. Men laughed as my assailant shouted, pained by the removal of hair from his head.

Then I saw Fairhair, his blonde locks framing a face that looked kind on one side, but deeply scarred on the other. The wound was old, but the cut had been deep and had left the left side of his face slightly misshapen. He smiled and reached out with his hand, encapsulating mine. They placed me back on the sand and the brute that had accosted me patted me on the head like a pet dog. I spat at him and pointed a curse. He responded by raising a hand, but was stopped by Fairhair.

'Leave her be. The night has wounded her enough, and she is angry. No one is to discipline her, but me, is that clear?'

Embarrassed by his scolding, the man nodded.

'Yes Lord,' he said and walked away. That part, at least I understood.

'Cinead,' Fairhair barked.

A gigantic man with beady eyes and long straggled hair jumped down from the ship and tried to run through the breakers, falling twice, much to the amusement of the others.

'My Lord?'

He spoke like the others, but it was not his native tongue. There was an accent.

'Tell the girl we will not harm her, that she is safe and under my protection and that we will take her with us.'

Cinead smiled at me as he spoke. I understood what he said, for he spoke my language, well almost; there were some differences. He was not an islander, but probably came from the mainland, where the accent was more diverse.

I shook my head defiantly and told him to go fuck a pig. He glared at me, more stunned than annoyed.

'What did she say?' Fairhair asked.

'Lord, she told me to go fuck a pig.' There were howls of laughter from the men who had now gathered around us.

'I will not leave my home,' I yelled. Cinead translated, and the response from Fairhair was blunt.

'What home? Your parents are dead, the village destroyed, you are all alone, child. They killed everyone; Cinead and I went to your village last night. There is nobody left. If any survived, they are long gone. Come with us and you will live, stay here and you will surely die. The choice is yours. I will not force your mind.' He turned to leave as Cinead translated. I hesitated, and Cinead could see my despair.

'He speaks the truth. I saw it with my own eyes. I'm sorry, but they're all dead. There is nothing left of your village. They burnt it to the ground. Come with us. He is an honourable man and will treat you kindly.' Cinead smiled and held out his pudgy fingers.

I looked inland, searching for a reason to stay, but there was none. We had travelled far during the night but I could see still see the smoke hanging like a death flag above my village. They were all probably dead, slaughtered like my mother, I thought. Fairhair was right. There was nothing here for me now, and so reluctantly I left.

I held Cinead's hand as we walked together towards the ship.

'I understand your pain,' he muttered. 'I lost my family, too. They weren't slaughtered like yours; I lost them to a sickness that took them all. My mother, father and my two sisters, it seems so long ago now and like you, I was just a child. I carry that hurt with me every day. It never leaves.' He paused, as if the memory was too painful to recall.

'But life goes on and we adapt to survive,' he added whilst

lifting me onto his shoulders and carrying me through the slight waves that lapped gently onto the beach. Several hands offered to hoist me on board, but it was Fairhair that pushed the others aside, lifting me gently and placing me onto the waiting deck.

He seemed relieved and pulled me close, holding me tight in what I could only describe as a loving embrace. I looked up at him and noticed for the first time how bright and blue his eyes were. He smiled down at me, as the sun pierced through the clouds that filled the sky; it bathed us in a moment of warm sunlight and he laughed.

I think he took that as an excellent omen, for he lifted me up towards the heavens. He was laughing and started bellowing something I did not understand.

'Odin, you have presented me with a gift so precious, a child with flaming hair and a heart just as fiery. I am so grateful and honoured by your kindness. From this day forth, she is Helga Haraldsdottir, and I ask that you watch over her and protect her always.' Men raised swords and axes towards the now blazing sun. I did not understand what was going on until Cinead explained it all to me later that day. I had lost my parents, my home, and now it seemed I had lost my name, too.

The ship lurched violently at first as it lifted on the incoming tide, then with each pull of the oars, the waves gave way until we were clear of the beach; my journey had begun.

The red sail caught the wind, and it flapped uncontrollably until it was full, joined like lovers in a billowing embrace. There was no coiled serpent on this sail; instead there was a yellow dragon that stretched out over a vibrant red background. I thought the dragon was beautiful, and it looked as if it was flying when the sail cracked and twisted, grabbing the easterly wind and forcing the boat to lurch forward. They placed me at the bow and I marvelled at the speed of the vessel as the sail urged us forward, slicing its way through white-tipped waves and hollowed swells.

There was another dragon; a head beautifully carved that sat proudly upon the prow. With scales, sharp teeth and a pointed tongue, it looked so fearsome and, I imagined, like the other ship that had landed on our isle, that it would strike fear in all who saw it. I turned and faced the shoreline as the crew strained and heaved on the wooden oars, dragging them on-board and plugging the oar holes. The wind was strong now and with a full sail; the ship sliced effortlessly through the waves; I stared and watched my island home slowly evaporate behind me, and I wondered if I would ever walk along its beaches again.

Ten summers I had spent on my island, I was but a child. A young girl that had been preparing her first offering to the goddess Brigid, and now my fickle deity had cast me out forever. I despised her, so I cursed and spat into the sea to cement my hatred. I would pray to her no more.

As the coastline drifted away, it overwhelmed me with sadness, but I would not give way to tears. Cinead, sensing my feelings, joined me.

'The Gods bring us a fair wind, our journey will be short.' He praised.

'Don't speak to me of gods,' I snarled. 'Mine has abandoned me. I am godless.'

Soon we were far out to sea and there was nothing left to look at. Cinead kept me company but did not speak, sensing my mood and need for silence. As my island passed beyond the horizon, he took my hand. Leading me back to the bow, we sat and watched as men sat sharpening their blades, singing a haunting melody with each stroke. Cinead explained the song was to appease the sea god Njord, asking him for calm waters and a safe passage home.

I had sailed before, several times, but never this far out to sea. I had only hunted fish in the shallows with my father in our small boat. Our fishing trips had been fun, full of laughter, and if the weather were clement, we would cook our catch on the sandy beach. Later, when the sky was dark and filled with stars, we would sit together and watch the heavens for signs of the Goddess passing us by.

My memories were tormenting me. I closed my eyes and buried my head in my folded arms, for I could bear it no longer. Cinead put a comforting arm around me and pulled me to him.

'I'm sorry, Helga,' he whispered.

'My name is Eithne,' I growled, pushing his arm away.

'Whilst in the company of these people, I suggest you answer to Helga, or your life could become difficult quickly.' He passed me some dried meat, which I eat gladly, realizing nothing had passed my lips since the Northmen had arrived the day before. It was salty, tough and made by jaw ache, but its flavour was pleasant enough and it soothed my growling stomach.

'We will reach land in three to four days if this wind stays kind. There will be a glorious feast when we get back. The likes you have never seen, ale will be plentiful and there will be much rejoicing. I can't wait.'

He seemed happy that he was going to wherever we were going. I felt distraught. A deep darkness had engulfed me, and my mind was awash with a deep loathing for everyone.

A warming sun travelled across the sky, scattering clouds as the gentle waves lapped against the sides of the ship. The song seemed to have worked for now, and I wondered if Njord really did exist deep below the waves. The sea was the quietest I had ever seen it. Maybe their gods listen to them, I thought.

As I sat and watched the men who had rescued me and brought me upon their vessel, I noticed how big and strong looking they were and how many had scars from fighting. Most had long hair and beards, and as my eyes scanned their faces, I noticed Fairhair. He was watching me closely. His scarred cheek made him look menacing, but his gentle blue eyes and twisted smile deflected his menacing persona. I did not smile back; instead I lowered my gaze and tugged at my knotted hair, pulling it apart and wincing at the process. Cinead had fallen asleep. His pig like snorts and inaudible mumblings would have been humorous on another day, but not today, for I kept seeing my mother's death over and over in my mind's eye. I wanted it to stop, to go away. All I could think about was her dismembered head staring, gawping; she had been beautiful, yet in death her face was so frightening. That is why, out of desperation, I jumped into the quiet sea.

The icy cold of the Northern waters stabbed instantly. It took my breath away and made me shiver. It was piercing, and I almost regretted my decision immediately. I wanted my life to end, and I was certain that would now happen. I felt fear, but it was fleeting. As the cold penetrated, I felt myself drifting away. It was so quiet and so tranquil. My sorrow was ebbing away, just like the tide that now carried me to my death. I shut my eyes and felt my consciousness slipping gently away; it was not an unpleasant feeling at all, in fact I found it peaceful. My senses slowly becoming numb, and I opened my eyes to look at the blue sky for the last time. Oh, how I wished the sky had still been blue. But clouds had now gathered, and instead there was a patchwork quilt of greys and black, a mirror for my sadness, I thought. I sighed and closed my eyes for the last time.

It was then I heard my Mother's voice.

'Eithne,' she called. I came alive instantly. The cold sea burned but my mother was calling and now I wanted to live, to find her in this desert of waves.

'Mother?' I screamed, searching the now swelling sea. The waves were bigger, much bigger than before. The wind had arrived and was whipping them up, painting white tips on the crested mounds that now threatened to engulf me.

'I am with you always.' She whispered; she seemed so close. I screamed for her again, over and over, but I saw nothing.

I tried to swim, kicking furiously against the powerful sea, but I was failing. Salt water choked me. As I sank beneath the growing waves, I knew I was drowning.

It was then I remembered Njord, and I screamed his name and begged him to save me. I no longer wanted to die. My mother had come to me and wanted me to live on. I had felt her presence, heard her voice. I screamed for Njord again and he saved me, or at least Cinead did.

'I've got you, Eithne. Hang on to me.'

I turned my head to see Cinead straining to hold me up and threw my arms around his thick neck; the waves were buffeting us violently, up and down in large swells. Water cascaded over us, and I gasped for air every time we surfaced. Cinead held me so tight around my small delicate waist I feared I might snap in two.

The waves kept reaching for me, their gnarled fingers trying to tease me from his grasp and drag me away.

I was tiring, and death was wrapping me up, offering an escape from the icy waters. I had no feeling; my extremities were already asleep as darkness encircled me like a hunting whale. Cinead sensed I was in trouble.

'Eithne, wake up, don't go to sleep, resist it. Your mother wants you to live, so open your eyes. Look, the boat, it's here.'

My eyes blinked open, and I watched as its dragonhead rose from the turbulent sea. Everything happened so quickly after that. Hands reached for us both and dragged us on board. They removed our sodden clothes and wrapped us both in warm furs. We were both trembling; we were freezing cold, but we had survived.

I clung to Cinead; he had saved my life whilst risking his own. I was sure I had heard my mother's voice, but now wondered if it had just been imagination. I had asked a god for help and he had sent Cinead to save me. It seemed destiny had not finished with me yet. I would live on and see where life would take me. I looked at Cinead and smiled.

'Never do that again, will you?' he scolded. 'If I have to die, I want it to be in battle, not drown in a freezing sea. Njord may want my bones, but it's Odin's hall I want to enter when I die and I don't want to be wet when I do, you understand?' I nodded, too cold to speak.

'We are your family now, Eithne. I know you have been through much and everything is strange to you, but I will help you adapt.'

Just then, a crack of lighting streaked across the clouded sky and a low murmur rumbled through the heavens. The boat rocked sideways, buffeted by the growling waves.

'I think your gods are angry. Maybe they wanted my soul.' I suggested, regaining my voice.

'Maybe,' said Cinead. 'Or perhaps they celebrate, thankful that we survived. Let's hope Thor sends light across the darkened sky to guide us home.'

'Who's Thor?' I asked as the wind howled and the rain poured. Cinead pulled me closer and cradled me in his arms.

He told me all about the God with the long Fairhair, who was the son of Odin, and wielded a magic hammer that made the lightning. He told me about Odin the All father, Loki the trickster God, and the goddess Freya who was beautiful and had a cloak of feathers that allowed her to fly across vast distances as a bird. I liked the stories and as sleep descended, I prayed that these gods and goddesses would not abandon me as Brigid had.

'Cinead?' I whispered drowsily.

'Yes Eithne.'

'Call me Helga from now on.'

CHAPTER THREE

'Helga, wake up.' Cinead was shaking me hard, and I moaned at being disturbed. My dreams had brought me some comfort. I had walked through fields of barley hand in hand with my mother, the sun was bright and the sea calm as we had stood on the shore watching my father fishing in the shallows. He waved, and we waved back. I was happy. Then Cinead's voice destroyed my vision and my happiness was gone, left behind, deep within the realms of sleep.

I was awake and my mood was as dark as the night sky above.

'What is it?' I growled.

'A ship, its been following us for a while now and draws ever closer. It is the men that attacked your village, Helga.'

'Will they attack?' I asked fearfully.

'We will wait and see what they want, but you must hide. In a ship full of men, you stick out like a sore thumb. Get in here,' he ordered. 'be silent and stay there until I come and get you.'

That's what my father had said, and a pang of worry struck at my heart.

They had lifted several planks from the deck and there was just enough space for me to squeeze between the chests, barrels and baskets that lay within the ship's belly. I lay flat and pulled my furs tightly around me. I was still naked underneath and complained as a basket grazed the only bare part of my leg.

'Be quiet,' Cinead growled, the planks replaced and a rowing bench placed upon them. He sat down on the bench and the timbers groaned under his weight. I was uncomfortable and unable to move. The air was stale and made more so when Cinead squeaked a rancid fart from between his blubbery arse cheeks. I complained loudly and cursed him. Someone stamped twice on the planks and growled at me again to be quiet. It

44

sounded like Fairhair, so I held my nose and listened intently.

It seemed like an age and my body ached because of my confinement; but eventually the ship came alongside.

'Jarl Heggalund. What a pleasant surprise. You have been raiding?'

'Jarl Harald, you have been raiding too, I see.'

'Not raiding, trading. A few supplies for the coming winter. If we don't have it, we buy it. Why make enemies if you don't have to? There are better reasons to die than for a sheep or some grain.'

I leant forward and pulled one fur to one side so I could see through the cracks and between Cinead's feet. Fairhair was smiling, but I sensed he did not like this person. His hand rested on his sword and his shield was nearby. The others seemed prepared also should this meeting go awry. I could not see the other boat or the man who was talking to Fairhair. However, I had heard the name Heggalund and wondered if he was one of those that had killed my mother.

'But if you take what you want; then your enemies fear you more. Try it sometime. We live by reputation Harald, only women buy things, not men.'

I heard laughter from the other boat and guessed he was throwing insults, because men reached for their shields and swords while others grabbed spears. Fairhair just laughed and waved his men to stand down.

'You are right Heggalund, women buy lots of things. They are costly creatures, are they not? But it is fortunate that I have so much gold and silver won in battle; that I can keep my woman contented. We are rewarded for our generosity; there is always plenty of humping in our village. Try it sometime.'

The men laughed loudly and although I could not see the Jarl's face; I imagined Fairhair had replied with an insult as well. 'Ahh, I jest Heggalund. Let's not quarrel. The gods sleep and if we wake them, they will be angry with us. They may send storms to spite us, and waves to crush us; we may never reach our homeland or see the women that cost us so dearly. My men are as tired as yours, I'm sure a warm bed and a beautiful woman is worth much more than turning the sea red for a few sheep or bags of grain, wouldn't you agree.' Fairhair wasn't smiling now and his hand still rested on the handle of his sword. His face had changed in an instant. The smile dissipated and instead was replaced by an icy stare and a fearsome grimace that would strike fear in most men. There was a moment of silence, but stern looks can speak a thousand words and Jarl Heggalund gave way.

'You are right Harald, maybe we can continue this discussion at a later date, in your village perhaps.' It sounded like a veiled threat, but Fairhair was unmoved. I heard a scrapping on the hull and guessed that the other ship was using oars to keep the boats apart.

'You are always welcome to visit us, Jarl,' he called, waving a hand nonchalantly. 'It would overjoy us to meet with you and your men. Bring your women too. Maybe they would like to buy some of our wares or join in the humping.' The men cheered and made rude gestures; which made me giggle. There was no reply as Fairhair turned away, and as the ships separated, Cinead stood and pushed up the planks, allowing me to crawl out of my hiding place. Stiff from lying squashed for so long, I stretched my arms and rubbed my numb legs and feet. Fairhair grabbed me and faced me toward the leaving ship. He whispered something in my ear and pointed. I did not understand at first until I saw the serpent sail and the man with the marks on his face.

Fairhair tapped his cheeks

'Hrafn,' he tapped his cheeks once more. 'Hrafn' he repeated.

Jarl Heggalund glared at us and I could see that the marks on his face were, in fact, birds, one on each cheek. This was the man who had killed my mother and destroyed my village. I stared at him, memorizing every segment of his being; I burned it into my memory and swore that every night before I slept I would think of him, see his face and then dream of the day I removed his head.

I nodded at Fairhair to let him know I understood.

'Raven,' I said, patting my cheeks.

'Raven,' he repeated, patting my head, which to this day annoys me.

Slivers of light appeared on the horizon, and I looked once more at the departing vessel.

I am not sure what came over me at that moment, nor did I care. I was ten summers old and felt rage in my heart.

'Thor,' I screamed to the heavens, my arms spread wide. My fur dropped from my shoulders and I stood naked on the deck of the ship. The men froze and stared at me as if I was moon mad.

'I demand my revenge. Let your hammer strike fear into

everyman on that ship.' I pointed, and the men looked.

'My name is Helga,' I screamed. 'Remember me when my time comes.'

A grumble of thunder crawled across the night sky and men muttered at what they took as a sign. I had asked, and Thor had answered; it disturbed them enough to look skyward in fear. The sky was clear, and the stars blazed bright, yet the thunder still rumbled, rolling across the heavens. I asked Cinead for his knife, but he refused, placing his hand over its scabbard. However, one other understood what I was asking for and stepped forward, offering me his seax. It was heavy in my hand and its edge was sharp as I ran it lightly across my hand. It sliced my palm easily and my blood flowed. I was about to dip my fingers into the pool that had gathered, but the man stopped me. I watched as he cut his own hand and placed my fingers in his own blood and placed his within mine. He smeared my blood across both his cheeks and then nodded for me to do the same. I did and knew we had both made a blood pact with Thor; it bound us together, and I smiled when I saw the hammer amulet around his neck.

'Thor,' he bellowed, picking me up and planting me on his shoulders.

The men echoed the call, and Fairhair was laughing joyously at my insanity. As we bellowed across the open sea, Jarl Heggalund looked back. I was sure that although it was dark, and they were now distant, he could still see a red-haired girl, pale and naked with a blade in hand, sitting on the shoulders of her Viking brother.

I cursed him, and all who followed him and knew that one-day our paths would cross again. When it did, I would kill him, or die trying. Another rumble of thunder cascaded across the sky, accompanied by a flash of light that reflected upon the rippling sea. I took this as a good omen, for the sky was crystal clear.

The rest of the voyage passed peacefully. Cinead regaled the conversation and insults of the night before and I laughed, thinking how clever and smart Fairhair had been. I found out the name of the warrior that had shared blood with me. Erik was young, maybe seventeen summers, brave and a fearsome warrior in battle, according to Cinead. He was a man of few words, lacked intelligence, but was blessed with fighting skills far beyond his years. He had stood in the shield wall and was a man I could always trust. I had made a friend and as I looked at Erik; he lowered his face, embarrassed because I was looking at him.

'He likes you,' uttered Cinead.

The day passed without incident. A fair wind blew steadily eastwards, and the waves pushed us gently forward. I sat near the dragon's head and gazed at the black and white whales that raced against us, disappearing and then rising again through the white-tipped surf. They were playing, and it occupied my mind as I watched them. My hand hurt where I had cut it, but I refused to have it covered. It had stopped bleeding and as long as I kept it still; it was fine. Erik kept me company and although I did not understand his words, I appreciated him being there.

'See, you have gained a brother already,' Cinead teased.

'So does that make you my grandfather, then?' Cinead laughed.

'Helga,' I looked round to see Fairhair approach. I stood up and Erik did the same.

He beckoned me to the side of the ship and pointed to the horizon. I could just make out a landmass jutting out of the sea, and I strained my eyes to see it more clearly. The light was fading as the sun continued on its westward descent, two hours light at most, I thought.

My feelings were all over the place and I didn't really know how I felt. I was worried and nervous. Fairhair sat and beckoned that I should sit beside him. Erik made to leave, but he invited him to stay. The man who had saved my life spoke softly, whilst stroking my crimson hair. I felt safe in his presence but unsure of my future and of the part he would play in it.

'That is your new home, Helga. You will be happy there. My wife will adore you. Asa will teach you to cook, weave, and sow. We will teach you how to make our sails and you will become a valued member of my household. We will treat you well. You are my daughter now, Helga Haraldsdottir.' He seemed so happy, as if he had found something he had lost a long time ago. 'You have much to learn, but first you must learn our language, and that is Cinead's job. He will be your teacher.'

And so it was. I had lost one mother and father and gained another.

How strange my world was becoming.

CHAPTER FOUR

It was dark when we arrived in Vestfold. The heavy rain stabbed my face and nipped at my hands and ears. So much rain, I thought, and it matched my mood. We had left the sea, lowered the sail and rowed with the tide up river. Hills and mountains loomed on either side of our watery path, their black shapes rolled like waves across the landscape. Vast expanses of trees peppered their sides, tall and pointed. I watched amazed '*so many trees,*' I thought. I had never seen so many in one place before.

Our progress was slow, but soon lights were seen flickering in the distance. As the river turned, bending sharply right like the hind leg of a dog, the men pulled harder, desperate to get home. Finally, and with great skill, they guided the boat into a sizeable docking area where several other ships, larger than ours, were tethered together.

People carrying torches ventured out to greet us, their smiles as the river we had just sailed. Most were family members, woman and children, but there were also warriors dressed in battle garments, carrying shields axes and spears. Some were young, but most were old, and as their torches flickered light across their wrinkled skin; it made them look fearsome and demon like. I shivered, not because of the cold, but out of fear and trepidation about my new surroundings.

I watched as children leapt into their father's arms and squealed with excitement, just as I had done with my father when he returned from his fishing trips. The rest embraced Fairhair, patting him on the back and thanking their gods for his safe return.

One took a particular interest in me. He was much older than Fairhair but seemed to be a man of some status amongst the group. His face bore the scars of battle and I noticed that his right arm hung in a weird and grotesque way.

'Who's this?' he nodded towards me and although fearful, I looked him square in the eye.

'This is Helga Uncle, she will stay with us.' Fairhair smiled at the man, but he was unmoved.

'A slave?' he asked.

'No a daughter,'

'Harald, you can't just replace one child with another. She is a slave girl and nothing more.'

'She is a daughter. A gift from Odin. We found her near standing stones and we watched her mother die a good death. She fought and died like a warrior Guthrom, like a Valkyrie, and if she has passed that spirit to Helga, then she will be a worthy daughter for my wife and I.' I could tell that the older man was not happy about my presence, he seemed uneasy and his tone was angry as he continued the discussion.

'All I see here is a wild child, look at her eyes Harald, she will bring us nothing but trouble. If your father was here,' he started; but never got the chance to finish. Fairhair became very animated and annoyed and made his feelings known.

'My father is not here,' he yelled. The throng of people hushed at his raised voice and turned to see what was happening. 'I care not what my father may have thought. He drinks and feasts in Valhalla with the gods now and although I value your guidance, this is my decision, not yours. If my father disapproves, then let him come to me in my dreams and tell me himself.'

The old man fell silent and reached towards Fairhair. They embraced, and the smiles returned.

'Let us not quarrel Harald, if your mind is set on this, then so be it.'

'It is Uncle, now lets not discuss this further; come let's eat and celebrate our homecoming.'

I watched as the two men walked down the jetty and turned

towards an extensive building that was much bigger than any other buildings in the village.

'Who's that Cinead?' I whispered.

'That's Guthrom. He is Haralds' uncle. A powerful man and a fierce warrior.'

'What happened to his arm? Was he injured in battle?' I was inquisitive. I knew the man disliked me and I wanted to know everything about him.

'No, it was not in battle and has nothing to do with you. It got crushed, so now he stays here and protects the village when Fairhair is away.'

'How did it get crushed?'

'Stop asking so many questions, just keep out of his way. His injury has made him very bitter; he's not a tolerant man, especially of youthful girls that talk too much. Now hush.'

I nodded to show I understood, but this man interested me and I wondered why Cinead was so reluctant to talk about his arm.

The village was so much larger than my own. In fact, it was almost three times the size, and more buildings were being built. I could smell fish being smoked nearby, another reminder of what I had left behind.

More people ventured out as the rain eased to a drizzle, and they soon filled the harbour with the sounds of laughter and cheering. Fairhair seemed well liked and a man of some status.

Suddenly, a woman rushed through the throng and threw herself at Fairhair; he picked her up and kissed her firmly on the lips.

A small, thin boy followed her. He stood patiently while his mother and father embraced, then smiled as he was picked up and placed astride his fathers' shoulders. I saw Fairhair whisper into the woman's ear; smiling she moved closer to me. The torches illuminated her red hair that curled around her face She had a kind face with deep green eyes and freckles that bridged her nose, but it was her flaming hair that caught my attention. Deep red, long and wavy, it looked just like mine, and I now understood why Fairhair had saved me.

I often wonder if he would have let me die had I been dark-haired or fair in colouring. I obviously reminded him of his woman, and that minor detail may just have decided my fate.

We strolled through the muddy streets and then entered a large rectangular building that was made mostly of wood, with mud walls and a thatched roof. A roaring fire sat in the middle, its smoke meandering upwards towards the hole in the roof. I had seen nothing as grand as this before; it was huge compared to my old home.

Cinead accompanied me to the fire, and I stood bathed in light and warmth as he removed my fur. My skin prickled at the heat and reddened instantly. A young woman handed me a linin undergarment to cover my modesty. It had long sleeves and hung almost to my ankles. They then draped a woollen apron over the top; it was beautiful, blue with straps that were fastened to the undergarment by two bronze brooches. Nobody noticed my nakedness, or if they did, they didn't care. Either way, they dressed me like all the other women in the room and Cinead said I looked sweet.

I sat with my teacher whilst he gorged himself on chicken and drank what smelled like ale from a wooden cup. Some of the women were looking at me; they smiled and two of them waved. I did not wave back; instead I averted my gaze, feeling awkward and exposed.

The Hall filled quickly, and the atmosphere was happy and raucous. They brought more drink and food to the tables, a collection of cold chicken legs, salted fish and pork were passed along the line and Cinead gave me a mixed bowl of meat, along with some bread, vegetables and a cup with a sweet smelling liquid. I ate heartily and watched as men talked and laughed, hugging their woman and children. It was a joyous scene, and for a moment, I forgot my woes and indulged in their festivities.

Fairhair stood and banged his drinking cup on the table; his woman and child were sitting by his side as they waited for the noise to subside.

'Well, I must admit it is good to be home,' he said, and the room erupted in agreement. He raised his hands, asking for silence before continuing.

'We had a wonderful journey. The gods blessed us with a fair wind and a calm sea… well, most of the time,' he added. His men laughed whilst nodding in agreement.

'We made some good trades, and the price was fair. As always, the people of the northern isles welcomed us warmly. They drive a hard bargain, but they have always seen us as friends, not enemies.' He poured some more ale into his cup and sat back in his seat. He grabbed Asa by the hand before raising his voice once more.

'So it disturbs me that others that visit from these lands were not so willing to trade, they only wished to take what they wanted and to do so in a murderous fashion.' He paused and looked straight at me.

The room fell silent and everyone stared; I lowered my head like the lost child I was and clung to Cinead tightly. He pulled me close and awkwardly ruffled my hair, whispering that it was ok. His voice soothed me, my native tongue comforting.

Moments passed; then I felt warm hands touch my face, sweeping the hair from my cheeks and lifting my head so I could see her face. Asa was so beautiful; her red hair, like mine, draped across her elegant shoulders. A beaded necklace hung around her neck and it twinkled in the quivering light. She noticed me looking at it, so removed it gently and placed it around my neck, kissing my forehead as she smiled, but it was a sad smile. My pain and loss were reflected in her eyes. She seemed to understand my sorrow and placed her forehead upon mine, as if trying to take away my grief. I could not smile back; I just looked into her deep green eyes and watched the tears form, then trickle down her freckled cheeks. She was crying for me, as she knew I had no more tears to give. She lifted me from Cinead's arms and, for the first time since my mother's death, I felt truly safe. I sat cradled in her arms with one arm around her neck, as I had with my mother not that long ago. Then she spoke to me through Cinead.

'You have nothing to fear from us, my child. The world may be a cruel place, but you have sanctuary here with us for as long as you wish it. My husband is a kind man; he's not like the ones who murdered your people. He's not like Heggalund.'

The name was enough to cause a reaction, and my expression turned from fear to hatred. She saw it, and it caught her by surprise.

'It's all right. He can't touch you here,' she said soothingly. I wasn't frightened, I was angry. I knew in my heart that I would find him one day. I would seek him out and kill him. I would cut up his body and scatter the parts so nobody could put it back together. There would be no burial, no pyre; he would be food for the wolves or bears, and the maggots would gorge themselves on his rotting flesh. His soul would never find peace. I would curse it and make sure it was forever in torment.

Something came over me, and it flooded me with rage. I started ranting in my native tongue. All the pain, sorrow, and hate rushed out of me like a screaming banshee. I became possessed by the need for revenge. Cinead tried to calm me, but I ignored him. Asa tried also, but they could not still me. She lowered me to the floor and glanced at Fairhair, thinking me mad. It scared them. I saw it in their eyes; I scared them all.

All except Fairhair; he stepped forward and slapped me so hard across the face that I tumbled backwards, hitting my head hard against a bench. That was the last thing I remember of that night. Seemingly, Erik had carried me to a bed and sat with me while the festivities had continued in my absence. He was still there when I woke and laughed when I rubbed my head where the bench had impacted. He made a fist and knocked on his head, then he knocked on the side of the wooden bed and I guessed he was comparing my head to wood. I smiled and slapped his arm so he hit me back… gently.

It was morning; the hall was no longer full of people, although a few who had overindulged the night before lay snoring and muttering in the befuddled sleep. Cinead was one of them, and the temptation to kick him awake was overwhelming. Erik stopped me and raised his hands like claws and growled like an angry bear. He shook his head, and I guessed he was describing how Cinead would react if I woke him up. Apart from Erik and me, there were only two others awake, both women who were bolstering the fire and clearing up the mess from the night before.

'Erik?' I asked. He looked at me and nodded. 'Teach me to fight.' His confused expression told me he did not understand. I looked around the building and saw a shield standing against a wall. Sauntering over to it, I picked it up. It was heavy, and it took an enormous effort to raise it off the ground, but raise it I did it. Erik muttered something, and then laughed, which annoyed me greatly. 'Teach me to fight, I screamed,' thrusting the shield forward, but Erik just shrugged. I put the shield down and pointed at Erik's seax. He took it from his belt and handed it to me nonchalantly. I returned to the shield, and with seax in hand, made a fighting pose. 'Heggalund,' I said, and finally Erik understood. He reached out and took back his seax, replaced the shield against the wall, shook his head, and walked away.

Sitting back on the bed, I rubbed my swollen head and contemplated the position I now found myself in. I was in a foreign land where only Cinead spoke my language; I was still a child and expected to behave like one, but most of all, I was a female. This had never been a disadvantage in the past. My future had always seemed so certain. I would have probably become our village priestess, at least while our people still revered our goddess. I may have married and had children of my own, cooked, weaved and helped with the harvest. But now I wished I was a man. For men can fight, they can stand on the battlefield and seek revenge. Well, I wanted revenge, and I was damn sure they would not deny me that privilege. In time, I knew I could persuade Erik to teach me, but first, I needed to communicate with these people so there was no alternative; I had to become Norse.

CHAPTER FIVE

Seven summers had passed since my arrival in Vestfold and I was no longer a child. I had tried hard to fit into my new surroundings and now spoke their language fluently. My ability to learn had impressed Cinead; but in truth, it was all credit to his teaching and patience, which I know I often tested to the limit.

I had grown accustomed to my new name and responded to it now without thought. I was proud to have the name Helga and the status that came along with it.

Harfagre and his woman, Asa Hakonsdotter, had taken me into their home, and as far as they were concerned, I was their daughter; although I think there were times they regretted that decision. The past years had been very hard as I struggled to adapt to this new life. I was lucky and privileged to live in such an esteemed household; I was a king's daughter, with all the trappings that entailed but at times, it was as much a disadvantage as a blessing. Many were jealous of my status and despised me for it, but some liked me, most of them men, which also did not sit well with the other women in our town. I didn't care; I knew they saw me as an outsider, and I suppose they would always see me that way. Most of the time I ignored them, but every now and again they would push me too hard and I would react violently, reshaping many a nose over the years, and now few dared provoke me. I had built a small reputation, and most of those of a similar age avoided me like the plague. I was like a hawk, small, fast, with extremely sharp talons.

I spent most of my spare time with men, listening to their stories, of places they had been and battles they had fought in, although much to my annoyance Asa made sure I indulged in the duties of a woman too. She taught me to cook, sew, and weave, and I now knew how to make my own clothes, although my attire was more like that of a man than a woman. Asa tried so hard; she made me beautiful woollen aprons in every colour imaginable, decorated with silk, an expensive addition for one so young. I had several pairs of shoes lovingly made over interminable winter nights and a hoard of jewellery and gifts from my father; brought from far-off lands by traders that visited during the summer months. I yearned to see these places for myself, but was always denied the chance to accompany my father beyond the confines of the river. I loved to sail and had a small boat of my own. Cinead and I used it to go fishing and to help me escape from my female chores. Although fun, I yearned for the open sea and all it offered, but for now my place was here in Vestfold.

I loved to fight. In fact, I craved it, and the more beatings I received, the more I yearned for it. I would watch the young warriors practicing their skills and then practice alone with a sword I had stolen from one of the boats. I would goad them and call them names, just to get a reaction, and when they responded, I revelled in the battle, usually coming off worse than my opponent. My skills were raw compared to the others, but it never stopped me trying and I was a fast learner. Cinead would scold me and Fairhair would give me chores as punishment, usually fixing sails or basket weaving, women's work, and I detested him for it.

'Give me a sword and shield' I would scream, 'teach me to fight.' But it always fell on deaf ears and I would swear and curse at him, which just made him laugh and give me even more chores to do.

However, I had one ally. Erik relented slightly; he grew tired of watching me taking a beating from the older kids, so agreed to teach me hand to hand combat just so I could defend myself better. It was fun and Erik was a master. I learned how to punch with power, use my speed and agility and kick where it hurts the most. I was a natural, spurred on by my deep-seated vengeance. It roared within my soul and every time I hammered an assailant; I thought of Heggalund.

Officially, Erik was teaching me how to ride; he was like a brother to me and I loved him so much. When he was home, he would take two horses from the stables and take me up through the valley to our favourite place. It was high upon a ridge that overlooked Vestfold. Surrounded by trees, the view was stunning, and I often thought about how different this landscape was compared to my island home. The wide rivers and mountainous ranges filled me with wonder. Yet when the biting winds swept in, bringing ice and snow from the North, it became such a cold and desolate place. When the first bite of winter whitened the morning grass, it was time to drag the boats from the river for repairs. Whilst the women sat around the fires, mending the sails damaged from the summer's journeys, the men would coat the hulls with tar and animal fat to protect them over the dark winter months. My job, of course, was with the women and I hated it. However, it did have its benefits. I loved the stories the woman told, giants, elves and dwarfs, magical cloaks and hammers, such wonderful tales passed down through the generations. It was here I learnt all about their gods; the dreary nights made ever shorter by the tales and exploits of Odin, Freya, Thor and Loki.

Winter had been challenging this year. The sun had been a rare visitor, and the ice had been reluctant to leave. But today there were the first signs that the spring tides had returned, the ice was melting, and the first shoots of spring had broken through the hard crusty earth. I loved this time of year and this one excited me more than any other, as Erik had finally relented to my constant nagging and promised to teach me sword and shield skills.

I woke early, unable to contain my excitement. I quickly dressed in my masculine attire and rushed outside to find Erik.

'Helga wait.' I turned to see Asa rushing to catch me.

'Take this with you. You have not eaten. I swear you will waste away, girl.'

'Thank you, mother,' I said, placing the bag over my shoulder.

'I will eat later, I promise.'

'Make sure you do. Now go find your father. He has a surprise for you.'

The streets were busy considering the time of day. It was barely light, yet small boats were already casting nets in the swollen river; the tide was full and a larger vessel was making ready to sail. I cast my eye toward the dry dock where another was being built. This ship was even bigger and was near completion. This ship was not for trade; it was a warship, the first of many. There were rumours of unrest beyond our borders, and my father was concerned enough to order several ships to be built to meet any challenge from the river or the open sea.

There had been many changes in Vestfold since my arrival. The once small town had grown in size, thriving under my father's rule. Strong defences had been built to protect its assets. Vestfold was growing ever richer. It was now a major trading hub and although with wealth came power and reputation; it also brought the risk of attack.

Trade had expanded both East and West, with ships now arriving every day from far-off places. A new palisade equipped with viewing platforms and towers gave us views far reaching into the lands beyond. My father had been busy politically too; his dream was to unite all the Kingdoms under one chieftain or king. He had been away for months, striking bargains with some, and fighting battles with those who had ambitions of their own. For those who pledged their allegiance, he allowed them to continue to rule their kingdoms on his behalf. These petty kingdoms paid taxes to my father, and for that, he guaranteed their protection and promised they would never starve under his rule. This promise he kept, and his renown, grew ever larger. However, there were rumblings of discontent further north and fears that my father was becoming too powerful. Cinead reckoned war was brewing and if the rumours were true, then the current peace would soon disintegrate.

I made my way to the stables where Erik was waiting; he had an enormous grin on his face and stood next to his usual mount; I was confused, as there was only one horse.

'Where's mine?' I asked.

'He's in there.' Erik said, gesturing towards the stables.

'He?' I questioned, as my usual mount was a mare. Erik had chosen her for me some three summers earlier; she was slow but sure-footed, with a gentle temperament, an obedient horse to learn with he had said; and that she was, but I believed he picked her because she lacked the swiftness of his.

'Off riding, are we?' Cinead asked, his red cheeks higher on his face than usual because he was grinning.

'Helga doesn't have a horse,' Erik replied.

'Oh, that's a shame. Ah well, maybe she could make me some new under garments for these have so many holes in them, look.' Cinead dropped his trousers and sure enough, they did.

I swore at them both for being so childish, which just encouraged them even more.

'Such language for a lady Erik, I wonder where she learns such words.' Cinead was shaking his head as if disgusted.

'I learn them from you when the ale has puddled your head, you are vulgar when drunk and you wonder why you have no woman.'

The last remark was hurtful, but Cinead just laughed.

The stable doors opened, and my father walked out, pulling behind him a beautiful white stallion. I had never seen such a beautiful horse as this. The only other visible colour was his grey muzzle and his light blue eyes. He was adorned with a blanket and fine saddle hand crafted from wood and leather.

'You like him, Helga?' my father asked.

'Yes, he's beautiful.' Was this the surprise Asa had told me about? I wondered. 'Is he mine?'

'Well, he's not mine, so I guess he must be.' My father had showered me with so many gifts before, jewellery mostly, but this was something far beyond what I deserved.

'Oh father, I don't know what to say.'

'Thank you would be good.'

'Yes, of course, thank you.' I flung my arms around his waist and hugged him tightly.

'Now we need a name for him. Any thoughts?'

'How about Curse Carrier?' Cinead mumbled under his breath, but just loud enough for us all to hear.

'I will call him Thunder,'

'I like that,' said Erik.

'A splendid name, Thor will be pleased,' my father complimented. 'Now jump up.'

I climbed upon his back and settled into the saddle. I took the reins from my father and patted Thunder on his flank. He threw his head up and down and stamped a foot; he was as excited as I was.

'Don't wander too far today. I have had reports of a small war band raiding in the east. I have sent out scouts, but as yet I've heard nothing. Keep watch and keep her safe, Erik. Asa would never forgive me if anything were to happen to her.'

'Yes Lord,' Erik nodded.

'And as for you,' he remarked, looking directly at me with a stern face. 'Do as you're told for once.'

'I will, my Lord.' I replied mockingly.

Pulling on the reins I kicked my heels and Thunder responded swiftly, like a streak of lighting from Thor's hammer he galloped away from the village. I turned to see Erik giving chase. He was screaming my name, and I laughed joyously.

I had never ridden so fast, and as Thunder's hooves rumbled on the drying ground, I almost squealed in delight. Even galloping uphill did not slow him down; he just changed his gait and charged onwards.

I had heard of the horses that lived in the northern lands; they were renowned for their speed and agility, and now I had one of my own; he was my warhorse.

We did not stop until we had reached the trees high on the hilltop where the deer roamed and the eagles flew. If ever the Gods visited our village, this is where they would sit.

Several moments passed before Erik appeared.

'Never do that again, Helga. How can I protect you if you ride off like that? You heard what your father said; you're my responsibility.'

'I'm sorry, Erik, but you have done the same to me plenty of times before. Thunder rides like the wind. I just got carried away.'

He sat beside me and we stared out towards the river.

'Do you miss your home?' He asked.

I looked at him and nodded. 'Yes, I do, and my parents.'

'Would you go back if you could?'

I had never thought of returning. For seven summers Vestfold had been my home, and I was content.

'Maybe one day, but only if you come with me.' I put an arm around him and pulled him close, kissing his cheek. Showing affection always made him uncomfortable, but I knew the feelings were mutual and, like a brother, he was always there for me.

The tide had almost turned, and the sun had retreated behind darkened clouds. There was a welcome chill that cooled us from the exertions of combat, and it pleased me that I had held my own against a seasoned warrior.

Erik waved his hand. 'Enough for today.' he had removed his

shirt, and I watched sweat trickle down the crease in his muscular back. I was exhausted too, and I was thankful when Erik halted our training session. I would never have asked to stop. To do that would make me look weak.

'You fight well now. Your skills are raw, but you have a natural talent, Helga. You have the heart of a warrior. Tomorrow I will show you some more moves, but we must keep this secret or your father will have me blood eagled.'

'Does she hump as good as she fights?' A voice spat from the tree line. He was tall, well dressed, and not alone. His eyes were narrow, and they ran across the contours of my body as he licked his lips like a hungry dog. Erik made a move towards his horse. It was grazing nearby and his shield hung invitingly from its side; but as he stepped forward, four others emerged from the trees and blocked his path. They stood together, hands on the swords, their shields draped across their backs. They were dressed for battle but looked unkempt compared to the other individual who had to be the leader of the group.

'I would suggest you stand down, boy.' He emphasized the word boy, and I could see a flame of hatred in Erik's glare as he took a step forward. I pressed my hand against his damp chest and felt his racing heart through my fingers tips.

'Don't Erik,' I whispered. 'They will kill you.'

'They will kill us anyway, and if I am to die Helga, then I will die fighting.'

'So, wench, what do you say? I've seen you fight. Why don't you come here and show me some of your feminine moves.' He smirked and the thought of his hands touching me made me think maybe Erik was right. Better to die than that. I stood my ground and Erik moved even closer to me.

'I am Helga, daughter of Harald Harfagre; if you're looking for food and ale and a place to rest, I am sure my father would be more than happy to oblige. Maybe then we can enjoy each other's company in more comfortable surroundings. I'm not one for humping in the open in front of others.' It was a futile attempt to diffuse the situation, and one I knew would fail.

'I know who you are, bitch. You are not a king's daughter, not that would matter anyway. You are no better than a whore. I will ride you like a dog, and when I'm done, they can have you next. Now strip and get on your knees, or should I strip you myself?' He unsheathed his sword and stepped purposely towards me as the others moved closer, too. That was a mistake, as he had underestimated the boy. What Erik lacked between the ears he made up for in battle sense. He was swift and skilled in the art of dispatching death. There were few better in the village and my assailant was dead before he could lay his hands anywhere near my youthful body. Erik pushed me to one side and side stepped the sword thrust before I had gathered what was happening. He grabbed the sword-carrying arm by the wrist with his right hand and with his left hammered against the elbow, there was a click and the tall man screamed, dropping his sword from his right hand. Before the others could respond, Erik used the sword to slice across his throat. His warm, sticky blood gushed, splattering across my clothes and face. I was shocked at first; the memories of my mother's decapitation came flooding back, but they were short-lived as I was no longer that little girl who had hidden in the trees beside the standing stones. I was Helga, I was Norse, and as a hairy arm encircled my neck, I lashed out.

Throwing my head backward, I connected with something. It was enough to make my assailant release his grip and as I turned; I noticed blood dripping from his bulbous nose. I also saw the knife in his hand, but he hesitated, standing his ground rather than attacking me. The others joined him; they had used the time to ready themselves with swords and shields. I was defenceless and vulnerable, but Erik stood with me, a wet crimson sword in his right hand. He had no shield, but strolled purposefully towards the four men. He seemed bigger, like a

God. Swollen veins pulsed in his arms and neck, and his blood-covered chest heaved with exertion and excitement.

'Go, go now,' he barked, his eyes large and glaring.

'No, I won't leave you,' I pleaded.

'Move,' he screamed. 'I will hold them off, get to Thunder and ride. Don't stop till you're home; do it now, Helga.'

And so I ran. One man tried to grab me, but Erik lashed out, allowing me to dodge the grasping hand. Thunder, sensing my urgency, raised his head from the lush grass and stood motionless as I leaped on his back and kicked my heels. The ringing of swords hitting shields was behind me. I quickly glanced back to see Erik fighting for his life. They outnumbered him four to one, but he fought with the arrogance and swagger of a seasoned warrior. I watched one fall as Erik deflected a blow and thrust his sword into the man's gut; but before he could remove his sword, they slashed him across his side. He staggered, almost falling; and the three remaining attackers charged at him head on. That was the last thing I saw.

Thunder leaped the stream that trickled through the valley. We raced down the track that led back to the town. Several men saw my approach, and I screamed for them to follow me and help Erik. My father and Asa were looking at the new ship and heard the commotion. They rushed towards me, thinking I was hurt. I was drenched in blood, and Asa began searching for a wound.

'I'm fine. It's not mine. They attacked us. Erik needs help, father.'

'How many?' my father asked.

'Five, Erik has killed two I think, but they hurt him father. You must hurry.'

My father wasted no time. He dragged me off thunder and set off. Several others grabbed horses and followed, including Cinead, who carried a cumbersome-looking battle-axe in his hand.

'Mother; Erik will be dead by the time they get there. He's hurt. I saw it.' I was panicking, and Asa tried desperately to calm me down, but I was having none of it.

'I need to go to him.' I was looking for another mount when a powerful arm grabbed me tight and spun me round. I protested, but Guthrom's grip was strong.

'Your going nowhere girl,' Guthrom held me tight with his one good arm and when I struggled, he pushed me back, pinning me against a gate. I just spat in his face and regretted it immediately. I expected retribution, but he just laughed and wiped my spittle away with his disfigured arm.

'Next time you do that, you had better have a sword and shield girl, the last person to do that I gutted and had his entrails scattered across a cornfield. Now stop yelping and get inside. Clean yourself up.'

'But Erik,' I protested once more.

'If Erik is dead, then he's in Odin's hall by now, drinking and celebrating a worthy death. If you learn anything from this girl, then be happy that Erik died with a sword in his hand and not with illness or old age. Only Hel's underworld awaits those so unfortunate.'

'Is that who's waiting for you, Guthrom?'

I was angry, not with Guthrom, but with myself. At my inability to defend myself and to fight alongside Eric, I was just a woman and still seen as needing the protection of men.

'Helga, that's enough.' Asa pulled me away. 'She's upset Guthrom. She means no offence.'

'Take her away, get her out of my sight before I do something I may regret later.' With that, he turned and left, and I knew I had hurt him far more with my vicious tongue than I could ever have done with a sword.

No one returned that day or the next. I had stood on the palisade hoping to see my father return with Erik and the others, but apart from visiting tradespeople selling their wares, I was left disappointed. *Why had they not returned?*

I spent some time practicing what Erik had taught me, hidden away from the busiest part of the town. I swung my sword at imaginary targets and blocked attacks with my shield. It was not the same without Erik, but it at least occupied my mind whilst I waited for word.

The light was failing, and the birds were singing a mournful song. It matched my mood. But then came a call from the palisade. Horses were approaching, and they flung the gates open to allow entry. Thunder raced through, weeping with sweat. My father looked weary and was dirt covered from his journey. The rest of the small band followed and I could see Cinead bringing up the rear, still carrying the battle-axe in his hand. At last, they had returned.

People gathered around the horses as I looked for Erik, but I couldn't see him. Asa forced her way through the throng and I followed.

'Father,' I shouted, 'Father.'

He heard me and lowered himself off Thunder's back.

'You look tired, husband, two days. We were worried.' It was a gentle attempt to scold my father for not sending word. He kissed Asa and smiled.

'There was no time to send a message, only urgency.'

'Where's Erik father?' I asked, fearing the reply.

'He's alive, but barely. He may not survive Helga, but he's in excellent hands.'

'Where is he? Why have you been so long? I want to see him.' I begged.

'We took him to Groa. He is with her now.'

'Who? Why have you not brought him home? I don't understand.' I looked at Asa, then back at my father. Again I asked, 'Who is Groa?'

It was Guthrom who answered, not my father. 'She's a healer, a Volva, and a good one. You were wise to take him there, Harald. If anyone can help him, it is she.'

'Is this true, Father? Is he with a witch?'

'Groa is many things, Helga. Many fear her, but she has the ear of the Goddess Freya and the wisdom of Odin. She will do everything she can. He's in excellent hands and if the Gods will it, he will survive.'

I had seen many men return from battle with injuries. They had taken none to a witch before, and as far as I was aware, this woman had never been to Vestfold, so I wondered why Erik had been taken to her; it seemed strange. My mind raced with thoughts and fears. I was convinced that Erik was dying and being prepared for his journey to Valhalla?

So, as everyone dispersed, I pulled Cinead to one side.

'Take me to Erik. I want to see him.'

'No,' Cinead shook his head several times and tried to walk away, but I pursued him, tugging at his arm.

'Take me or I will go myself.'

'You don't know the way, so let it be,' he snarled.

His abruptness took me back. He was weary, I could see that, but I would not relent.

'You're are frightened of her, aren't you?' Cinead looked skywards.

'Helga I will not take you. Your father would forbid it, and I don't intend to test his patience on this matter. You would be wise to let this go.'

'Cinead,' I was pleading. 'Would you leave my father on a battlefield?'

'What?' It took a while for my point to sink in, but when it did, he replied.

'It's not the same,' he said sympathetically.

'It is the same.'

'I left Erik to face them alone. You all see me as a woman in need of your protection, yet all I have ever wanted to do was fight; shield to shield together with you, Erik, and my father. I left him behind Cinead, don't you understand?'

He stared at me, and I knew he did, for I could see it in his eyes.

'Let me be with him now,' I continued. 'If he is to die, then I want to be there. I will make sure he goes to Valhalla. I don't want Hel to take him to Nifelheim.'

He looked at me, and he could see my pain. He realized I was wounded too, and that my guilt was almost too much for me to bear.

'I would do the same for you, Cinead.'

I was desperate, and I knew I would never find Groa alone. Cinead was the only person who might consider taking me, and even that was a long shot.

'Would you let me die alone?' I asked.

Cinead dropped his head and stared at the earth. He rang his hands through his hair and cussed.

'Your father will gut me for this,' he whispered.

'When do we leave?' I smiled, kissing his cheek.

He thought for a while before answering.

'There is a gathering tonight, a feast with lots of ale that I will now miss because of you. Your father has invited the local Jarls to discuss the attack against you and Erik; he wants the men found. We did not recognize the three we found dead; their shields bore a pattern unknown to us. The other two had escaped by the time we had arrived; Erik must have fought valiantly against such numbers. If he lives they will die, if he dies they will suffer.'

I had not realized the seriousness of the attack, or the political consequences that might lie ahead. My father was a fair man, but such an attack against me was, in his eyes, far beyond his tolerance. They knew who I was and where I would be. This was not a random attack. It seemed they had planned it and had almost succeeded.

'When you can, make an excuse to leave; I will follow you out,' Cinead explained. 'The main gate will be open for our guests. It will be guarded, so I will distract the guards whilst you make your escape.' You will be on your own, as it will take me time to gather a horse and give chase. The guards will inform your father of your actions, and that I have set after you. You can explain yourself to him on your return. I will meet with you as soon as I can; wait for me where the river splits in two, just beyond Odin's throne. You know the place?

'Yes, I do.' I knew the way, but I was uncertain I could find it in the dark.

'Good; arm yourself and take a shield too, sling it over your back and try to look like a warrior. When you get there, don't light a fire, just stay put until I find you; any sign of trouble, hide, you understand?' I nodded, listening intently.

'If I'm not there by daylight, find somewhere safe; well hidden but high enough that will allow you to see my approach, or the approach of others. You are sure you want to do this? Erik protected you; I feel like I'm putting you at risk.'

'I'm certain' was my simple reply.

'All right, then. Do you have questions, Helga?'

'No, just don't be too long and stay sober.' I joked, but in truth, I was nervous. I had never ventured beyond the safety of the palisade on my own before. This would be the first time and my self-confidence wavered. I felt anxious; but the thought of Erik stirred me, making me more determined than ever to be by his side. I had chosen my path; I just hoped I had chosen the right one.

CHAPTER SIX

Asa had enquired why I was leaving and where I was going, but accepted the excuse that I needed some air. The heat was making me feel queasy; I had said. It was so hot in the meeting hall and the spit roasting pig added to the humidity. She had offered to accompany me, but I told her there was no need, I would be ok, and was just going to walk to the stables to feed Thunder, which in part was true.

The cool air was welcoming, and I thanked the Gods for a moon bright enough to guide me on my journey. It was late, and the streets were eerily silent as I made my way towards the stables. Once inside, I saddled Thunder and prepared to leave. I had taken a sword, shield and the means to carry such items from one of the boats earlier in the day and had hidden them in the stables. The shield was old and its design faded; it still bore my father's dragon, but it was hard to see, and I doubted that it was noticeable from a distance. The sword was plain in design but was comfortable in my hand and had a good edge. It would do.

I exited the building with Thunder and walked towards the gate. There were a few small outbuildings nearby, so I waited there, hiding in the shadows just out of sight of the men that guarded the gate. The gate was open, as Cinead had predicted, and as he approached, the two guards waved and greeted him warmly.

'All quiet, I take it?' asked Cinead; noticing the ale the men had tried in vain to hide from him.

'You won't say anything, will you, Cinead?' one guard pleaded.

'No Ulf I won't, but these are dangerous times my friend. You need to be more vigilant, the smell of battle is in the air, and it creeps ever closer. Now pour me a drink.'

With the guards distracted, I made my move. I climbed onto Thunder's back and raced past them before they realized what was happening.

'That's Helga,' I heard one-man shout, but before he could raise the alarm, I was out of sight and galloping northwards. My heart was racing, and I was now alone with only the moon and stars for company. There was still an icy chill in the air as the last remnants of winter stubbornly pinched at my face and hands. The ground was soft and in darkness I could not judge the undulations; so once out of sight of Vestfold, I reined Thunder in. The last thing I needed was a lame horse.

The journey to Odin's throne was slow and uneventful. I had travelled this path once before with Erik, but that had been during daylight hours, at night every hill and tree looked the same and at times I felt I was travelling in a circle. However I managed to navigate my way without getting too lost and now I was sat silently beside the slow-moving river, waiting for

Cinead to arrive. It was getting colder as evening passed into early morning. I was thankful I had brought my hooded cloak; the woollen garment comforted me and gave me warmth as I pulled it tightly around my body. I searched the horizon for any sign of an approaching horse for what seemed like hours. My eyes were heavy, aching for sleep, my head lopped forward and I was about to wander into the world of dreams, when I heard voices chattering from across the river.

'Get up bitch before or I whip you raw.' I could see nothing but heard the screams.

Cinead had told me to hide at the first sign of trouble and I did consider it, but the sound of more shouting stopped me from leaving. Someone was in trouble, and although I could see no movement on the adjacent riverbank, the voices could be clearly heard above the trickling river.

'Get up and move, I won't tell you again.' A mans voice snarled.

'Stop hitting her Gudlaug, mark her and the gold will turn to silver.'

I could not judge where they were, but they had to be close by. I was concerned they would see Thunder under such a bright moon; so I led him to higher ground away from the rivers edge and tied him to a small tree before returning to where I had been sitting.

'She might have a golden body Kvist but she has the stubbornness of a mule.' I heard Gudlaug curse, and the girl wailed once more when he hit her again, I felt my anger rising in my chest but I stayed put.

'Enough, we will make camp here, a few hours' rest won't hurt. Oddvar and the others will find us soon enough, I'm sure. Now make a fire, it's cold.'

'Is that wise someone might see it?' Gudlaug remarked.

'It will help Oddvar find us, just do it there's nobody else mad enough to be out here.'

Kvist's words worried me. How many others was he talking about and where were they? Could they be on my side of the river? I was racked me with indecision, and I feared Cinead might run into trouble on his way here to meet me.

I watched as the first sparks flashed in the darkness; flames followed and before long, a fire blazed brightly, illuminating the individuals that now huddled together around its warming glow. I could see the two men, but could not see the woman. Their attire suggested wealth; they both carried swords, and I noticed two shields laying nearby, propped up against a broken tree. These men were not warriors though, their attire was not that of someone that would stand in the shield wall, no these were traders; not of goods, but of people, and the woman was obviously for sale and had been promised to someone very important.

Their description of her was strange though; I would not describe most of the slaves around here as having a golden body. Most would be lucky not to be scared or pot marked. This woman had to be special if the whip had to be restrained to keep her price intact; I was intrigued.

I shivered as the chilly breeze stung my face and yearned for a fire of my own. Cinead had said no fire, and now that one burned so brightly on the other bank, I hoped that if he saw it, he would not think it mine.

Where was he? Why was he taking so long? Maybe he had run into trouble or, even worse, maybe he was dead. If something had happened to him, it would be my fault; my stubbornness to be with Erik might have cost Cinead his life; try as I might, I could not extinguish these dark thoughts from my mind.

'Helga.'

I jumped and grabbed my sword, which was ridiculous, as my assailant had called me by my name.

'For the love of Thor Cinead, you nearly stopped my heart.' I whispered. Then I saw Guthrom with the horses. 'What's he doing here?'

'He saw you leave, he's come to take you back.' Cinead lowered himself down beside me and watched the men over the river, avoiding my gaze.

'I'm not going back until I've seen Erik.' I spoke to Cinead, but looked at Guthrom. He ignored my protestations and joined us.

'I know them,' Guthrom muttered. 'Where are the rest of them?'

'They expect them to join them soon. Why?' He did not answer but murmured something into Cinead's ear.

'We're leaving. Grab your things,' Cinead barked.

'I'm only going one way,' I argued.

'That's where we're going girl, now get on your horse.'

Guthrom's response surprised me, and I wondered why the sudden change of heart.

'What will happen to the girl?' I asked.

'What girl?' Guthrom growled.

'They have a girl I heard her crying. The one called Kvist said she is valuable.'

'Bastards, Guthrom cursed. What else did you hear?'

'Just their names; Gudlaug and Kvist. Another called Oddvar is the one they're waiting for but I think he has other with him, but I don't know how many.' I looked at Guthrom, who stared blankly.

'Guthrom, we must leave. It will be light soon enough. We should slip away while we still have the cover of darkness.'

Guthrom glared across the river towards the two men, then looked at Cinead. I jumped on Thunder's back in preparation to depart, but Guthrom stayed motionless.

'You go, take Helga with you, I will catch up,' He ordered.

'What's going on Cinead?' I asked.

'Those men are slavers, they trade in women, young girls like you.' He explained.

'I had already figured that out. Tell me something I don't know.' Cinead said nothing. He just stared at me blankly.

'They took my daughter.' Guthrom blurted. In an instant, his face showed the pain and loss he had endured at the hands of these men. I was shocked and slipped off Thunder's back. Cinead replicated my actions and the two of us stood searching for the right words.

'You knew about this, Cinead?' I asked. He nodded before answering.

'Yes, that's why we go north now, to protect you; better that than run into Oddar and his men on the way home. He does not want the same fate to befall you that happened to Svanhild. But he won't leave the girl, not now he knows she's there.'

'Guthrom, what are we going to do?'

'You're going to do nothing girl, I will get her out of there, you do as your told and go with Cinead.'

'No… I spat in defiance. I will never leave anyone alone

again. If you plan to do this, we do it together or not at all.'

Guthrom looked at me for a moment, then nodded. 'So be it but you do as I tell you.'

'Agreed,' I smiled.

CHAPTER SEVEN

It had been ten summers since Guthrom's daughter had been taken; three summers before my arrival in Norvegr.

Svanhild had been playing not that far from where Erik and I had been attacked. Hilde, Guthrom's wife, had been collecting wild garlic when the group appeared from the woods. It was an opportunist and violent attack. Moving swiftly, eight men on horseback had exited the woods. The lead horseman knocked Hilde to the ground with the edge of his shield, and as she tried to get back up, the ones that followed savagely cut her down.

Svanhild ran screaming, but the man on the lead horse gathered her up into his hefty arms, and galloped away at speed. A single person had witnessed the attack and raised the alarm, but by then Svanhild gone and had never been seen again.

My father had sent men in every direction to look for the abductors, and although rumours were plentiful and the names of Gudlaug and Kvist prevalent, they failed to find them.

A visiting trader had told my father, that if they were trading in slaves, they were probably heading for Hedeby in Danmork; or further still, Dyflin in Ireland.

Not long after that, Guthrom had travelled to Hedeby with two men in an attempt at finding his daughter. What he found instead was trouble. Traders of people dislike interference in their businesses and took exception to his questioning. One evening, as they searched the taverns for Gudlaug and Kvist, they were set upon. Only Guthrom survived, although he often wished he hadn't. They took him to a small building, stripped him naked, and tied him to a cart. There, he met the two men he had been looking for. Kvist enjoyed beating Guthrom. His whip cut deep across his chest and his punches almost made Guthrom unrecognizable; but that was nothing compared to the damage the blacksmith's hammer did to his right arm. By the time they had finished, the arm was almost severed. He had lost consciousness and when he had come round; it was daylight. They had left him; thinking he would die an excruciating death, but Guthrom was strong and refused to die. The gods had been watching and took pity on him. The owner of the cart did what he could before bringing him to Vestfold. Like Erik, he was taken to Groa, who saved the arm, but it was so badly deformed and weakened by the injuries that he now struggled to raise it above his chest. Guthrom had lost his wife, his daughter, and the use of his shield arm.

I now understood the reasons for his bitterness. We had more in common than I thought. He had never liked me, thinking me wild and unruly, but at that moment I felt only pity for him.

'Lets kill them,' I spat.

'Not before they tell me where my daughter is,' Guthrom whispered. 'Cinead and I will handle this, you will stay here.'

'No, I will find the girl and take her to safety and then keep watch for the others. You don't want Oddvar arriving unannounced.' Guthrom reluctantly agreed, seeing my reasoning, although Cinead was far less enthusiastic.

We had to move fast as the first signs of dawn were now stretching lazily across a brightening sky, but it was still dark enough for us to implement a surprise attack. Cinead had tied a shield to Guthroms' crippled arm; he could still use it but could not grip the handle well enough with his shattered hand. Guthrom was left-handed and Kvist and Gudlaug had mangled the right, thinking that would be his sword arm. That error could prove to be a very costly mistake.

Cinead led the way, and I followed at the rear. I was nervous but Erik had trained me well, and I was more than confident in my abilities, should the need to fight arrive.

It took a while to traverse the river; fortunately the tide was turning, so the water was moving slowly. It was relatively

shallow where we crossed, but in the darkness, one wrong step
could cost us. A slip now could not only cause injury, but could
alert the enemy to our presence. I helped Guthrom keep his
shield above the ripples, much to his annoyance. Raising it
above his head was almost impossible, and even with my help,
it was still difficult. He grunted his frustration as we forged
onwards.

As silently as we could, we exited the water. We were three
against two, but I was no warrior, and Guthrom was disabled. I
had never seen Cinead fight and worried his large bumbling
frame could be a disadvantage. It now seemed like utter
madness to be doing this, but doing it we were.

My heart was pounding like a blacksmith's hammer and
although I did not fear death, I feared the process.

I drew my dagger, which calmed my nerves, I felt Erik was
beside me, whispering advice. I kissed the blade softly and
asked Thor for guidance.

Cinead moved fast for a big man, crashing through the undergrowth like a rampaging bull. Kvist reacted quickly, reaching for his sword and shield, but the beast was upon him before he had the chance to ready himself. Cinead slammed into him, knocked him headlong into the fire. Sparks danced in the cool night air as he rolled free from the scorching flames. He attempted to rise, but the point of Cinead's sword was already at his throat, and he yielded quickly.

While all this was going on, Gudlaug never moved. He just sat motionless, chewing on a strip of dry meat. He stared at Guthrom and recognized him immediately.

'I remember you,' he smirked. 'How's the arm?'

Guthrom smiled, but I knew the slur had cut deep.

'I want information and if I like what I hear, I might let you live.' He said calmly.

Gudlaug nodded, and showing an open hand, said.

'Come, sit by the fire lets talk. It will be dawn soon and I love to watch the night turn to day. It's so pleasing to watch the colours reappear upon the land, don't you agree.' He was stalling, knowing that Oddvar had to be close by.

'A gracious gesture, but we are in a hurry. Now either you tell me what I want to know or I will slit you in two right now.' Guthrom smiled. 'Your choice,' he added.

Gudlaug's persona changed. He spat out his chewed morsel and got to his feet, reaching for his sword and shield. Guthrom stood motionless, as if relishing the challenge. I took a step forward, more in support than action, but was halted by Guthrom's sword arm.

'Step back girl, I've got this.'

Gudlaug was a brute of a man, tall and strong, with forearms bigger than my thighs.

'They don't except cripples into Valhalla, you know,' Gudlaug teased, hoping to goad Guthrom into an attack.

'Maybe so, but it's only warriors that can enter Odin's hall, so I guess that rules you out too.'

Gudlaug took the bait and raced towards Guthrom. I watched transfixed as Guthrom first neatly sidestepped the blow, then swiftly sliced his sharp blade across the back of Gudlaug's knee. He yelped like a scolded puppy and dropped to the ground.

'Helga, you will never see the likes of this in a shield wall. He is only good at killing defenceless women and stealing children. He is of no use in an actual battle.' Again Gudlaug responded; rising to his feet, he aimed a blow at Guthrom's head. It was a weak attempt and easily defended. Their swords met, and although Guthrom was disadvantaged, he was highly skilled and seemed to enjoy every minute of the encounter. He ignored several chances to finish the fight, preferring to indulge himself in combat, as if not wanting it to end. Every time they came together, Gudlaug suffered a cut or a bruise.

'We don't have time for this,' I shouted, 'Kill him, the other one will tell us what we need to know.' I pointed at Kvist, and Cinead nodded in agreement.

'Your right, I was getting bored anyway.'

Guthrom moved forward, grimacing. I had never seen him like this before; I imagined him before his injury, younger and stronger, standing with others on the field of battle.

Gudlaug tried to defend himself, but he did not have the required skills. His death was swift and much quicker than he probably deserved. Clutching his throat, he fell to his knees, blood tricking through his grubby fingers. He did not see the final blow coming, but his staring eyes acknowledged his defeat as he fell.

Guthrom turned his attention to Kvist; blood dripped from his blade. As he approached, I saw fear reflected in Kvist's eyes.

'I will tell you what I know, everything, whatever you need,' he stammered. 'Please don't kill me.'

Remembering the girl, I left Guthrom and Cinead with Kvist. Venturing towards where their horses had been tethered, I found her; bound and gagged to a nearby tree. As I approached, her big brown eyes starred at me and I raised my palms to show I meant her no harm. Reaching down, I unfastened the gag around her mouth and untied the ropes that encircled her wrists.

'Who are you?' she asked. I was surprised she spoke our language, as she was obviously not from our lands. Her hair was black like a raven, and her skin was indeed a golden brown. I guessed that she was older than me, but not by much.

'I'm Helga, daughter of Harald Harfagre. You have nothing to fear from us.'

'I am Manara,' she whispered, her voice quiet as if not wanting to be overheard, 'I'm a slave.'

'Not anymore, you are safe now.' I grabbed her hand and pulled her upright. We returned to the others, but not before I had untethered a strong black stallion for Manara. He was a handsome beast, and only someone with significant wealth could have afforded such an animal.

'Can you ride?' I asked.

She looked at the horse, and her worries evaporated. 'Yes,' she replied, her voice quiet and respectful.

'Good, he is yours then.'

Manara cried; tears rolled down her cheeks as she fell to her knees and kissed my hand. I felt awkward and dragged her upright once more.

'Stand up, Manara, you don't kneel to me or anyone else. You're free now, but we must leave before the others arrive.'

'Oddvar is a demon. You should be wary of him, Helga, avoid him at all costs.'

I did not respond, but I took her warning seriously; the thought of him seemed to terrify her. I led Manara to where the others were.

Kvist was unfortunately still alive, although looking slightly worse for wear.

'Helga, go fetch the horses, he's coming with us,' ordered Guthrom whilst binding the hands of our prisoner.

'I will go,' and before I could respond, Manara had leapt onto her horse and galloped off across the river, returning swiftly with our horses.

'Where does a slave learn to ride like that?' I enquired.

'Where I come from we ride before we walk.'

'Lets get moving.' Guthrom commanded

As I climbed onto Thunders back, I smiled at Manara. I liked her already and felt there was more to this girl than meets the eye. Together we rode along the river before crossing and continuing our journey northwards.

The dawn had broken, but it was dull, a blanket of inky clouds covered the entire sky that whispered rain. We had a head start, but knew that Oddvar and the others would soon follow. Cinead had extinguished the fire, but fingers of smoke still clawed their way through the canopy of trees. They would find Gudlaug's body down by the river and would demand recompense, but I also knew that it was Manara that they wanted more. As a slave, she would command a hefty price; one that Oddvar would not be willing to give up lightly.

Reaching higher ground, we scanned the horizon looking for horses, but saw nothing. Kvist said that Oddvar had over fifty men in his band and by killing his brother; we had made a dangerous enemy. Guthrom knew that was an exaggeration. It would be more like thirty at most, he reckoned.

We moved as quickly as we could, hoping to lose them in the mountains. The higher we climbed, the more difficult the terrain became, so we dismounted and walked, picking our way up the narrow pass. Our slow progress made me nervous, and I continuously looked behind us, expecting at any moment to see our pursuers appear on the narrow trail.

'Where are we going?' Manara asked.

'To see a witch,' I replied.

She gasped, and in a language I had not heard before, muttered what sounded like a prayer.

'Don't worry, the Gods will protect us.'

'Your Gods may protect you, but what about me?' She murmured.

'If they refuse, then they will be no longer be my Gods.'

She smiled and together we climbed.

CHAPTER EIGHT

The ascent seemed never ending; higher and higher we climbed into the mountains. The clouds met us and a light drizzle dampened my hair. Visibility was poor, and even the sure-footed Thunder found the climb difficult.

'How much further is it?' I asked. My back ached and my legs burned and I knew Manara was suffering the same, as she grimaced and groaned with every upward step we made.

'Once over this rise we drop again, it's only another half a day's ride from there,' Cinead replied.

Manara whined, but we pushed on relentlessly, step by agonizing step. After a while, the narrow track widened and levelled out. It was a relief when we finally reached the top. The view was awe-inspiring; this truly was a beautiful land; even through the mist, I could see the trees stretching out, carpeting the landscape as far as my eyes could see. The river we had crossed earlier meandered snake like, along the valley floor, slowly turning and making its way to the open sea.

It was then I saw men on horseback I counted around fifty; they were in no hurry as they crawled along the far side of the riverbank just below us. Guthrom saw them, too.

'Do you think that is Oddvar?' I asked.

'No, I recognize those shields, they're Jarl Heggalund's men. I wonder what they are doing here. They rarely venture this far south.'

'Heggalund? That is the name of the man I was promised to.'

'Is this true,' Guthrom asked Kvist.

Kvist smirked but did not answer; he just shrugged his shoulders.

Guthrom took a step towards him, and Kvist reflected the step backwards.

'I won't ask you again, I will just kill you.' Guthrom

threatened.

Kvist looked towards the horsemen before replying.

'Yes, we promised her to the Jarl and maybe those men are on their way to meet up with us. Once they have found out what you have done, they too will come looking for you. It seems you may have made yet another enemy, my friend.' He laughed, and I snapped.

I was within arm's length with my knife in hand when Cinead grabbed me.

'Let me kill this piece of weasel shit. We don't need him,' I growled.

'No, he may yet prove useful.' Guthrom barked.

'He told us he knows where Svanhild is.' Cinead whispered. 'Guthrom believes he speaks the truth. But no amount of beating or threats will prise that information from him; it is his only bargaining chip, so for now he lives.'

I relented, and Cinead released his grip on me.

'He knows nothing Guthrom and will say anything to save himself. He is like the worm that wriggles under your foot. The more you press down, the harder he wriggles. Any friend of Heggalund is my enemy.' I spat towards Kvist.

'Heggalund is not my friend,' he sneered. 'He is a customer, nothing more, and she belongs to him.'

'Kill him, Helga,' Manara urged.

'Enough of this,' Guthrom snapped. 'Nobody is killing anyone, we will rest here until they pass.' He beckoned Cinead, and the two men withdrew some distance to talk. This I found annoying and something I could not ignore.

'Don't pretend that Manara and I are not a part of this.' I shouted. 'If you have something to say, then say it to all of us, we are not children.' Guthrom turned to face me.

'Ha,' he spat. 'But you are a child Helga, you're selfish and lack respect. You let your emotions guide you and you put others in harm's way. I warned Harald, when he brought you to

Vestfold, that you would be trouble. Now, because of you, we have to creep around hoping to avoid a confrontation. You should be with Asa stitching garments and repairing our sails with the rest of the women and children not out here risking our lives just to get your own way.'

I responded without thinking, angry at the accusation, even though part of what Guthrom said was probably true.

'Were it not for me you would be still wallowing in your own self-pity, thinking your daughter lost forever. Now my selfishness has given you hope, you should be more grateful. And as for being guided by emotions, isn't that what you're doing too?'

The back of Guthrom's hand stung my cheek; it was a powerful blow, full of anger and sadness, and I probably deserved it.

'Stop,' Cinead shouted, glaring at both of us.

'This is not helping our cause. We have more important

things to deal with.'

Grabbing my arm, he pulled me close.

'Watch your tongue Helga. I swear it will be the death of you. And as for you Guthrom, strike her again, and by Odin's hand, I will cut you down.'

I had never seen Cinead so angry; he was always been so mild-mannered and gentle. He pushed me away, and I withdrew with Manara. Guthrom said nothing and returned to watching the riders pass by.

'You don't like him, do you?' Manara asked, nodding toward Guthrom.

'No, he thinks I'm a weak and childish girl that should know her place.' I spat.

'Is it possible you misjudge him? Maybe he just wants to keep you safe, after all, he knows how it feels to lose a daughter. Perhaps he doesn't want your father to feel the same sorrow.' I looked at Manara and sighed.

'I don't know, he's never liked me. He doesn't understand why I'm the way I am. Erik does; he is the only one that truly understands what I feel in my heart. I cannot bear the thought of loosing him.'

Manara put a hand around my shoulder and I swallowed my emotions. No tears, not today.

'You should not be so harsh on her Guthrom.' Cinead whispered, thinking I could not hear.

'She will get us killed Cinead, she's too unpredictable.'

'Maybe she is, but you weren't there when we found her. Think of your own pain, my friend; losing your wife and daughter strikes you deep, does it not? Is Helga's pain less heartfelt? She was but a child Guthrom. Unpredictable she may be, but her will is strong and her loyalty unquestionable. She has a warrior's heart and would die for her cause, just as you would. She has much to learn, but scolding her is not the way she needs our guidance.'

Guthrom did not respond, but looked in my direction. I pretended I had heard nothing and attended to Thunder, stroking his ears and patting his side gently.

We watched as the men below drifted southwards, finally vanishing into the trees far below us.

Guthrom grabbed the reins of his horse and ordered us to move. The five of us carefully meandered our way down the hillside and onto the valley floor below.

The clouds followed us downwards and hung heavily, trapped within the valleys walls. The Rain increased in intensity and Guthrom thanked the Gods for the shitty weather. It would be harder now to traverse the slopes as we had done earlier, thus hampering our pursuers slowing their progress. It was a slight advantage, but one we were thankful for.

The rest of the day we continued north, staying close to the tree line in case others crossed our path, and we needed a place to hide. The ground was uneven in places and slippery from the wet conditions, so we still had to take care as we inched our way towards Groa's cave.

The weather remained murky and damp, we were all soaked to the skin and the icy chill penetrated my body and made me shiver uncontrollably. My red locks lay flat against my head and back, and my skull and neck ached. Manara was even worse off; her bare arms and legs were pimpled and her teeth chattered. She seemed ill prepared for such a climate, and I feared for her health.

I reined Thunder in and drew up alongside Cinead, who had Kvist for company.

'We need to find shelter. Manara is freezing out here.' Cinead looked at the girl and nodded. He urged his horse into a trot, leaving me with the reigns of our prisoner, who smirked at me.

'You're all going to die out here.'

I ignored him and watched as Cinead joined Guthrom at the head of proceedings. Guthrom looked back and said something to Cinead, then galloped off, disappearing over a slight rise that obscured my field of view.

'Where's he off to?' I shouted.

'If he's got any sense, he will leave you here. Maybe he values his life above yours.'

Kvist never saw my punch coming and although it was just a backhanded clout, it was enough to break his already crooked nose; the blood flowed and his words ceased.

'There is a small farm nearby where we can seek shelter and get warmed.' Cinead explained. 'Heggalund controls this land, but many of the people here are poor and starving. A little silver might persuade them to let us rest for a while. It's a risk, so stay alert.'

We dismounted and waited. Cinead stripped Kvist of his leggings and jacket and passed them to Manara, who slipped them on over her own clothes. She looked comical in the oversized attire, but they would at least help to keep out the chill. Kvist, whose nose still wept, spat a curse at us, which amused me.

I removed my blade and saw a glimmer of fear appear in Kvist's eyes. Removing some dried meat from a pouch attached to my saddle, I cut into it; offering a few slices to the others. I heard rather than saw Kvist's sigh of relief.

'You know that he will say anything to save his life don't you Cinead? He's a slimy turd.'
Cinead stuffed the meat into his mouth and attempted to reply.

'Maybe so,' he mumbled. 'But until Guthrom is finished with him, he lives.'

Kvist smiled at me. He was pinning all his hopes for rescue on Oddvar's arrival and was juggling his usefulness until then. Guthrom believed his bullshit, and I feared that might cost us dearly, although I understood his need.

It seemed like an age before he reappeared. He waved at us to follow him; so once more, we mounted our horses and tracked through the valley to join him.

'I have scouted the area, and it seems safe enough for now, but we should remain vigilant. I have given coin, and the farmer has promised us food and a place to bed down for the night. I told him we were travelling north with slaves for the Jarl.'

'Slaves?' I questioned. 'What slaves?'

Guthrom smiled as he tied my hands and removed my knife, repeating the process with Manara, who held her hands out readily. I wondered how many times she had faced that indignity in her life.

'You will fetch a handsome price, Helga,' he joked. I ignored him and scowled at Cinead, who just lowered his gaze. Kvist found it hilarious until Cinead tied the gag around his mouth to stifle his amusement.

'Keep quiet and say nothing. I will answer for you if questions are asked.' Manara and I nodded.

For all my embarrassment I knew for this ruse to work, I

would have to keep quiet. Quite a challenge, I thought, but the

promise of food, shelter and warmth would help to seal my lips.

CHAPTER NINE

To say the place was a hovel was an understatement. It lay hidden between two wooded areas on a plateau halfway up the side of a hillock, not the best position for a farm, as when it rained, like it had today, the sloping ground flooded causing it to become boot deep in mud.

Cinead unbridled the horses and led them to a small paddock where they could graze on what little grass there was to be found. There was also a trough of water, and Thunder made straight for it.

'I have some feed for your horses; you're welcome to some for a small token of gratitude. My daughter will feed them for you if you so wish.'

I did not trust this man. He was sly looking, like a fox, with narrow eyes and a crooked smile. I saw him looking Manara up and down and heard him say to Guthrom what a fine specimen she was; he disgusted me and my gut screamed that he was trouble. I noticed a young girl staring at us from the doorway of a small outbuilding. She was so skinny, almost emancipated. Her hair was matted, and her clothes torn and dirty. I guessed this was the daughter he was talking about; she looked to be around eight summers old. Her gaunt eyes stared at me and I smiled, but there was little response, she just turned away and went back inside.

We all made our way to the main building. It was small, barely enough room to fit us all in, but at least there was a fire, and it kept out the damp and cold that had plagued us all day. Guthrom made an act of pushing me to the floor roughly; he was enjoying his new role as a slave master, so I spat in his direction, playing my part. He smirked and repeated the process with Manara, who didn't respond at, all she wanted was the warmth of the fire.

'What's his story?' Asked the farmer, gesturing toward Kvist, who had been placed in a dark corner as far from the fire as possible.

'He's a thief that was sentenced to lose his hands, but I intervened, offering a small payment for his crimes. He will make a good slave. He's sturdy enough but has a snakes tongue, hence the gag. I was thinking he could work the land, once tamed.'

'I see you have already started his training,' he smiled, noticing the facial bruising and blood stained cheeks.

'You said you have food,' questioned Guthrom, changing the subject.

'Fish from the fjord, small but nourishing enough, wait here I will fetch some from my smokehouse.' As he left, I noticed he glanced toward Manara, licking his thin lips.

'This is a bad idea we should leave,' I whispered. Manara nodded in agreement.

'I don't trust this man,' she added.

The farmer returned carrying several fish and his daughter had bread; it was not much, but Guthrom thanked him for his hospitality and began conversing with him about his farm and the inclement weather. Manara and I sat silently and listened as Cinead dozed, snorting pig like in front of the blazing fire. Guthrom untied our hands so that we could eat. The fish was delicious and once devoured. He put our restraints back in place, although fastened loosely.

'What about him?' The farmer enquired, gesturing towards our prisoner.

'Until he learns to behave, he doesn't eat.'

There wasn't enough room for us all to sleep in the one dwelling, so Manara and I were given quarters in one of the more dilapidated outbuilding. We were slaves, so a small barn and a few chickens for company was a luxury for our kind. Our legs had been tied together to keep up the pretence; Guthrom had taken us there and had returned my knife, placing it inside my boot.

'Just in case,' he whispered before leaving.

Kvist was taken elsewhere, so that Guthrom and Cinead could keep a close eye on him. Manara and I cuddled together for warmth it was cold but at least the building was watertight as the heavens opened once more. As we listened to the rain tapping on the roof, my eyes became heavy, I was so tired and with our bellies full and our clothes now dry, sleep devoured us both quickly. My last thought was for Eric.

'Please don't die.'

I woke in a panic; my face was being slapped hard, I screamed out as I tried to fend off further blows. It was still dark, and I was drowsy and slow to react.

A hand was placed over my mouth to silence my agitation. I fumbled for my knife but stopped when I realised how small the hand was that covered my lips. I was disorientated, as I had been lost in the world of dreams, conversing with my mother; I cursed the interruption, as her words were now lost to me in the waking world.

The girl pointed, and I noticed Manara was missing. I had heard nothing and cursed the fact that I had slept so deeply.

I reached for my knife and swiftly cut away my restraints. Seeing my blade, the girl panicked and jumped back, preparing to run. I held up my hand.

'Wait, I won't hurt you, what's your name?'

'Hella,' she replied quietly.

I smiled, removing the rest of the binds around my hands.

'I am Helga. Where is my friend?'

'He took her,' she whispered.

'Your father?' I asked.

'He's not my father. You must hurry, I will take you, I know where they are.'

We left the outbuilding together, and I followed her across the muddy yard and down a trampled pathway way that led to the woods. Thankfully the rain had ceased, but the air was damp and the cold chill cutting.

'Quickly this way,' Hella urged.

We ducked under low branches and quietly crept along the track; careful not to step on anything that would alert the farmer to our presence. Fortunately, the damp had seeped far enough into the ground to dull any sounds under foot. Muffled voices reached my ears, and I raised my head slightly to take a look. Although dark I could just make out the farmer, who was hunched over, whilst seemingly being annoyed at something or someone. It was then I saw Manara. She was lying on her back, her hands still tied in front of her, but her feet were now untethered. She was kicking and thrashing as her assailant tried to spread her legs apart. An owl screeched in the distance, and a memory took me home, back to the stones and my mother. I lost her forever, and I was determined not to let history repeat itself.

I turned to Hella. 'You stay here. I will try to get closer. When you see me wave, stand and scream as loud as you can to get his attention. I will do the rest.' She nodded to show she understood, so slowly and carefully, I made my way towards my quarry. Like one of Freya's cats, I stalked him, merging with the habitat, using every bush and shadow I could find to remain unseen, until I was ready to pounce.

Manara was now naked below the waist and the farmer was fumbling with his trousers. He seemed to be holding a knife to her throat, so I understood why she had stopped fighting back.

Gripping my knife tightly in my sweaty hand, I made ready to attack. I was nervous, but Erik's training had served me well in the past, and I was confident this skinny turd of a man was no match for me in a fair fight. However, he was armed, and I would have to deal with that threat first.

I raised my arm high and Hella screamed. The high-pitched

shrillness caused hidden animals to run in panic. A deer bounded by, adding to the confusion. As the farmer turned towards the scream, with his knife raised and ready to defend himself, I leapt from cover and rushed him from behind, He heard me coming and started to turn, deflecting my lunging knife but not preventing me from knocking him to the ground. Luckily the impact knocked his blade from his hand and I kicked it away before he had a chance to retrieve it.

He rolled and jumped to his feet, more nimbly than I had expected. Not as weak as he made out, it seemed.

'What do have we here?' He spat. 'I suspected as much, slaves my arse. Your ruse didn't fool me. Sit down girl and wait your turn, I will fuck you next.'

Uncontrolled anger made me attack, and I immediately regretted my decision. He was quick and easily ducked my knifed fist, lashing at me with a flailing hand that caught my midriff. It was the slightest of blows, but enough to wind me, causing me to crumple hopelessly to my knees, where I felt the full force of his boot against my face. My head shot backwards and although dazed, I was still conscious enough to drag myself from further harm. I swore internally for my arrogance, I would have to be more careful.

I turned to Manara, who had got to her feet and was trying to remove the binds from her wrists with her teeth.

'Run,' I croaked, but she stood her ground, shaking her head.

The farmer had found his knife, and we circled each other, both looking for an opening and a chance to strike. He attacked, stabbing towards my chest. I easily sidestepped his thrust, pushing the arm away. As his body turned, I elbowed him hard. I heard the snap of a rib and he fell backwards. I threw myself onto him pinning his knife-wielding arm with my leg, whilst stabbing towards his throat. He tried to fend me off with his other hand, but several strikes made it through, and his warm blood gushed and spurted over my knife wielding hand. He bucked like an unbroken horse and gouged at my eyes. As I turned my head, he managed to grab my wrist, twisting it hard. I gasped with the pain and dropped my blade. Leaning forward I bit his hand hard, breaking the skin. He immediately let go, allowing me to pummel his ugly, wizened face with both my fists. He wasn't finished though and reaching up with his blood-soaked hand he grasped my throat. His grip was powerful making it hard for me to breathe. Reaching up with both hands, I attempted to release his vice like grip. I was starting to gasp for air and darkness began to descend. He gurgled a laugh and sat up as I fell backwards. That's when Manara struck; moving swiftly; she placed her tethered hands over his head and dug her fingers into his eyes, pulling back as hard as she could until his head was trapped against her breasts. He cursed and thrashed as she struggled to hold him there. Kicking and twisting frantically, he tried to escape but Manara held firm. He released his grip on my neck and air rushed in, but before I could react, my knife was thrust into his chest. It was a vengeful blow, filled with power and hate. She stuck again and again in what was a frenzied attack. White eyed and open-mouthed, he gurgled his last breath as his head lopped forward. Hella was still ripping at his chest, stabbing and tearing. She was a silent killer, no noise or scream, just vengeance surging through her delicate frame. It was at that moment I wondered what horrors she had faced at the hands of this monster. I reached forward, gathering her into my arms, pulling her close, just as my mother had done to me when I had need of it. I looked towards Manara, who was sobbing; her hands still round the face of our assailant. We just sat there together, the three of us, covered in blood.

Almost unnoticed, Guthrom appeared, sword in hand. Hella's scream had woken him up and he had rushed to find us. For the first time in my life, I was actually pleased to see him.

CHAPTER TEN

'Burn it,' ordered Guthrom 'Burn it to the ground.'

'Someone will spot the flames.' Cinead interjected.

'Hopefully, Oddvar, by the time he gets here, we will be long gone. It may help put more distance between us.'

I could tell Cinead was less than convinced, but he followed Guthrom's instructions and the farm was soon ablaze. 'What about the girl?' He asked.

'She comes with us. We don't want any loose ends. Helga and Manara can look after her.' Guthrom looked at me and I nodded in agreement. Hella was clinging to me like a limpet as Manara and I prepared the horses. I lifted her gently onto Thunder's back, where she sat still and silent, her eyes staring at her bloody hands. There was no time to clean ourselves off. We had to leave straight away.

The sun powered through the clouds as we left, a welcome change from the cold and wet of the day before. I wrapped an arm round Hella and urged Thunder forward. My mind wandered. Half a day's ride, I told myself, soon I would be reunited with Erik and I prayed to the Goddess Freya that it would not be too late.

The rest of the journey was without incident, and I now understood why it had taken so long for my father to return to Vestfold. This place was no easy trek, and the last climb to reach Groa's cave was arduous and could only be achieved on foot. It must have taken a monumental effort to carry Erik up to this place.

Guthrom had stayed behind with Kvist and the horses whilst the rest of us made the strenuous climb. Cinead placed Hella on his shoulders and brought up the rear, his strength and determination never failing to amaze me.

I imagined Guthrom wanted to spend more time alone with Kvist, hoping to extract more information about his daughter's whereabouts. I was dubious that he would learn anything new.

By the time we reached the plateau, I was soaked, this time not by rain but by sweat. My mouth was dry from the exertion, making it hard to swallow. My limbs screamed and my head pounded. Manara had fared much worse, weighed down by garments two times her size. She bent double and tried to vomit, but nothing was forthcoming. I pulled her to her feet and pointed to a small stream that tumbled over nearby rocks before disappearing downwards to the lands below. This was obviously the start of a river, and I wondered if this was the same river we had crossed days earlier. We both knelt low, cupping our hands and devouring the icy cold water before cleaning off as much as the dried blood that clung and stained our skins. Cinead placed Hella next to us but drank instead from a leather water carrier. He was panting, but seemed unperturbed by the steep climb. His overweight frame did not seem to hinder him at all.

'Where did you get that from?' I asked.

He smirked before replying.

'I carry it always. I prefer to know where my water comes from and not chance disease or illness.'

Manara muttered something under her breath in her strange tongue. I guessed by her expression that it was aimed at Cinead and reckoned it defamatory.

'Why are you here?'

I turned to see a tall, lithe woman, hooded and cloaked in grey. A wolf stood obediently by her side; its yellow eyes transfixed on us all, its lips curled and nose shortened as it took an aggressive posture.

Cinead stepped forward, but stopped immediately as the wolf moved towards him, its hackles now raised high upon its back.

'Groa, it is I Cinead, we have come to see the boy.'

'Ahh, I remember you, you came with Fairhair.'

It surprised me that she called my father by that name, as that was what I called him as a child.

'He paid me well for my services, do you?' Cinead baulked at the question. He had not realized that payment might be required. He stumbled over his words, so I intervened.

'I am here to see Erik and I won't be denied by you or your wolf; does he live?'
Groa exploded into laughter.

'Ah, you must be Helga. I have heard many things about you, child. Your impudence offends me, be gone before I set Gunnolf on you.'

'I'm no child witch, and I don't fear your wolf either. So if you want to keep him, I suggest you let me see Erik.'
I had come this far and was not backing down now, 'I will leave after I have seen my friend not before.'

'Don't anger her Helga, she will curse us,' Cinead begged. I ignored him and continued.

'Well, what is it to be? Do you want to keep your pet?'

'I was told you were a feisty one. Come then, if Gunnolf decides to let you pass you can enter.' With that, she turned away, disappearing inside the darkened entrance, leaving the wolf to stand guard.

I stood rigid for a moment, staring at the enormous beast that stood before me. His Bright yellow eyes with black marbled pupils stared me down, daring me to advance. He curled his lips again and growled a sneer.

'Come on Helga. Forget it. She doesn't want us here and I have no coin.' Cinead grabbed my arm, but I pulled away.

'You go, I fear no dog and who is she to order me about.' I was spitting mad and stepped purposefully toward the entrance of the cave. Gunnolf's nose shortened even further, as he bared his white fangs and cautiously took a step towards me.

'Helga,' Manara whispered. 'Stare him down, move slowly, and don't avert your eyes from his. You must show no fear or weakness. If he moves towards you, then you do the same, show him you are the more powerful.'

'Do you want to come with me?' I asked.

'No, I will stay here with Cinead.' She smirked, urging me forward.

And so I did what Manara suggested and eyeballed the creature that stood before me. He was frightening and as I crept forward; he took a step sideways, still growling.

'Look, he's frightened of you,' shouted Manara.

'Or he's trying to out manoeuvre me so he can rip my throat out.' I was tempted to run, but resisted the urge. Instead, I turned towards him and scuttled crablike towards the entrance of the cave. Again, he circled me, and each time I adjusted my position to face him directly. I was almost there when Groa appeared.

The piece of meat arched through the air before landing at Gunnolf's feet.

'Lie down,' she barked, and the Wolf obeyed her instantly. 'You are a persistent brat, aren't you? Well, you had better come in before he finishes that morsel.'

I didn't hesitate and followed Groa into the cave. It was bigger than I thought, more like a cavern than a cave. It was warm inside, with a small fire that sparked and spat in one corner. I watched as a smoke trail meandered towards the roof, where I noticed a small natural hole in the rock that sucked out the grey curls, keeping the cave smoke free. It was dark inside, and it took a while for my eyes to adjust to the dimness.

'Sit,' she barked, bending down towards the fire. I found a small bench and lowered myself gently. 'Not there,' she spat. 'Over here by the fire.'

'Where's Erik?' I asked, as I could see no sign of him and worried that I was too late. Groa ignored my question as I sat next to my host.

She placed more wood on the fire and poured a liquid, which I guessed was fish oil, onto it. I watched mesmerized as the flames danced and cracked, rising upwards filling the cavern with a glorious orange light. It was then I saw Erik, hidden in a recess deep within the cave. As I moved to get up, Groa grabbed my shoulder.

'He sleeps deeply, leave him, he's fine.' Her tone had softened, and I did as she asked.

'He's not dying?' I asked.

'Not if the Gods do not wish it, and my understanding is that they don't.'

'Praise be to Thor,' I whispered, and Groa smiled.

'I think it is Freya you should thank, for it is she that has saved him, not Thor.'

'Can he talk?' My question prompted more laughter from Groa, and for the first time, I noticed her features. She was not how I had imagined a witch would look like, and I could not understand why men feared her so. Her laugh was infectious and her face lit up like a winter's moon. For all her age, beauty still lived on her face and I imagined that in her younger years she would have courted many suitors.

'Your name was first on his lips Helga; you have a bond with my son. He offered his life for you and you have risked yours by coming here.'

'Your son what do you mean?' It confused me.

Groa poured me a drink, and as I lifted the beaker to my lips, Gunnolf approached. My heart thudded in my chest as the wolf drew closer. Groa watched with interest as he padded over to the fire and lay beside me. I was speechless as the animal placed his head in my lap and nuzzled my hand. I hesitantly placed my hand on his head and stroked it gentle. He licked my fingers and my heart retreated to a more steady rhythm.

'You must be a special child,' Groa smirked. 'That's two of

my children you have bewitched.'

CHAPTER ELEVEN

Groa's story was tragic. Daughter of a Jarl in the barren ice lands, she fell pregnant to a young warrior named Erik. She had been promised to another, to help forge an alliance and strengthen further her father's position of power, so when he heard of her condition, he was livid. He executed her lover cruelly and cast her out.

'You have no worth to me now,' were his last words to his daughter. Although many had urged the Jarl to reconsider, including her mother, he remained steadfast and refused to discuss the matter further.

She left home on foot, with meagre rations and very few clothes, and would have surely died in the winter months if fate had not intervened. For as she wandered, hungry and cold, two sisters that were foraging in the icy lands for herbs and grasses, found her and took her in. These women, believing she was a gift from Odin, taught her the ways of the Volva and together they left the icy lands, moving gradually south, eventually finding the cave where I now sat.

The two women had helped her through her pregnancy and the birth of her son. The delivery was a tough, and Groa almost died from the blood loss. Exhausted, she passed out. But not before naming him Erik after her beloved. Then, as she slept, one sister took him away and she would never be a part of his life ever again, until now.

To be a Volva, there must be no distractions and this cave is no place for a child, they had told her. Groa pleaded for her son to be returned, but the sisters refused, promising he was better off where he was. He would be cared for and would prosper with his new family. Groa never forgave the sisters, but realising her son was lost to her, she dedicated her life to learn everything she needed to know to become a Seidr. Skilled in magic and the art of healing, her reputation grew and word spread of her skills and insight. She received invitations to the halls of powerful men and women who wanted advice and guidance in war and marriage. On her travels she had searched for Erik but never found him, not until Harald Fairhair brought a wounded warrior to her for help. She knew it was Erik when she saw the heart-shaped birthmark on his right wrist, and the resemblance to her lover was unmistakable. Twenty summers since his birth, and now Groa had her son back.

'I'm so sorry,' was all I could say.

'Odin saved my life, but took my son as payment, and now Freya has brought him back to me. There is no need for sorrow. What about you Helga?' She looked at me and I almost felt her stare burying deep into my soul. 'I see the fire of anger in your eyes. It floats in a sea of deep sadness. It's so bright it engulfs you. You yearn for revenge and one day you may have it, but at what cost?'

'I care not about the cost as long as I can kill Jarl Heggalund and avenge my parent's death.' I was steadfast and snarled with contempt.

'You care about nothing else? Just revenge?' She asked not waiting for my answer. 'It eats away at you, and it will tear you apart if you're not careful. Maybe you should trust in the Gods more and let them decide your destiny and that of the Jarl.'

Her words angered me. 'Listen witch,' I spat. 'Heggalund will die by my hand or I will die trying, do you understand me?'

'Your mother was a priestess.' It was not a question, it was a statement, and I was shocked at first, but then figured Erik must have told her at some point.

'Yes, she was.' I replied, my ire decreasing.

'She is happy that you have found a new home and family.'

I did not respond.

Groa sat silently for a while, looking into the fire.

'I'm sorry,' I sighed.

Groa smiled. She reached out and clenched my hands.

'The Gods decide our fate Helga, not us mortals. Your mother died bravely, I see it in the flames, but I do not see your father there. Maybe he still lives.'

Could that be true, I wondered?

'The village was destroyed, everyone was dead.'

'I said he may still live; I do not see him in the fire like I see your mother. I see many things, yet your father eludes me and your future is uncertain. Your anger may be the reason the clouds hide your destiny, that or there are choices to be made before your path is clear. You put your trust in Thor, but we have many gods and goddesses Helga. You should not restrict yourself to just the one. For each serves a purpose, and even Loki the trickster can have his uses. However, it maybe people that help you more than any of our deities.'

'Like Erik?' I asked.

She smiled. 'Like Erik, yes, but many more will come into your life, many you can trust and some you cannot. The skill is to tell them apart. You can't do this on your own child. You must learn many things over time and with the help of others. you could become an exceptional leader of people, but only if you allow the clouds to part.'

'What about Heggalund?' I asked.

'The Gods can be fickle.'

Her words stirred my memories. I had thought the same when I was journeying to these lands as a child. How strange that she used this expression now.

'Get some rest, you have a lengthy journey ahead of you. Drink this, it will help you. relax.'

Sleep descended like a sinking ship, drawing me down into the depths of slumber, dreams, and nightmares. I knew I was sleeping, but the visions seemed so real. I was wandering a battlefield and there were so many bodies lying dead or dying on the blood-covered ground. Beyond the slaughter, there on a mound made of skulls and bone, and upon it stood a woman. She wore a hooded cloak of feathers that seemed translucent.

'*Your father is waiting for you.*' It was my Mother's voice, but this was not my mother and I stared with disbelief as she morphed into some kind of hawk and flew skyward.

'Mother,' I yelled.

Light streamed into the cave, and I realized it was daylight. I was confused, as it felt like only moments had passed.

'Helga, it's all right, you were just dreaming.' I recognized that voice immediately and jumped to my feet. I almost knocked Erik over as I leapt at him, throwing my arms around his broad neck.

'Ouch steady Helga, I still hurt you know.' He was smiling, his face battered and bruised, but smiling. I let him go and stepped back. It was then I noticed his injuries and gasped in horror.

'Oh, Erik, look at you.' His torso was a mass of deep cuts and bruises, and I wondered how anyone could have survived such injuries.

'It looks worse than it is and I have the witch to thank for my life.' I looked at Groa, who shook her head, Erik did not know that the witch was, in fact, his mother.

'I thought you were dying. I came to make sure you had your knife with you when you entered Odin's hall.'

'You needn't have bothered; I still have my sword.' He laughed, then winced, and I embraced him once more but gentler this time. He lifted my head from his bare chest and kissed me tenderly on the forehead. 'Thanks for coming, I love you.' I almost cried, but swallowed it away; that was the first time Erik had verbally conveyed his love for me. It was a moment I would cherish always.

Our moment was brief as Cinead, Hella, and Manara rushed into the cave. Gunnolf jumped to his feet and emitted a low gurgling growl. A single command from Groa stopped him in his tracks, and he sat obediently as I stroked his head.

'What's wrong?' I asked.

'We have company,' Cinead replied. 'Looks like Oddvar has finally found us,' then he saw Erik and concern turned to joy. 'You have seen better days, Erik.' Erik nodded in agreement as Cinead warily stepped past Gunnolf and embraced his comrade.

'Who is she?' Erik asked, gesturing toward Cinead's companion.

'That's Manara, she's with us, we rescued her, I will explain it all later. Can you ride Erik?' Cinead nodded towards the terrible wounds unsure if his friend could suffer being jostled about on the back of a horse.

'If needs must.'

Erik stepped into the darkness of the cavern and returned with his sword and jacket. 'Thank you, witch.'

Groa watched Erik leave without saying a single word.

'Groa, come with us.'

She shook her head solemnly.

'No this is my home, Helga; I know no other. Take this with you. It contains a healing balm. Use it sparingly, morning and night. Erik is a quick healer, and this will assist his recovery. Don't let him ride for too long, as his wounds may open up again, and don't let him fight, unless his life depends upon it.' She hesitated for a moment as she wiped tears from her eyes.

'Keep him safe for me.'

'I will try.'

'Now go quickly, but leave Hella with me.'

'What?'

'Leave her here with me. It's meant to be, the Gods demand it.'

'Why?'

'Don't question the will of the Gods child, and remember

there is always a price to pay. Now go.'

I hesitated and looked at Hella.

'We haven't time to debate this, Helga.' Cinead barked from the entrance of the cave.

'All right,' I conceded. I grabbed Hella's hand, and she obediently followed. 'This is Groa. She is a going to look after you now.' I kissed her forehead. 'Be good and listen to what she says, for she is wise and a friend of the Gods.' Hella nodded but did not speak as I exited the cave.

I left, not knowing if I would ever see Groa and Hella again. A dark feeling niggled deep within me and as I started my decent, I began to worry. I looked back; but all I saw was Gunnolf standing alone, watching me leave; his whining the last thing I heard as he dropped out of sight. Groa's words haunted me. What were the Gods planning and would be the price?

The others were waiting for me at the base of the cliff; they were all mounted, and I noticed Manara sat behind Erik on her black stallion. Kvist was the only one on foot, and I wondered why.

'Hurry Helga,' Guthrom barked.

'What about him?' I asked, pointing at Kvist, who smiled at my arrival.

'We're leaving him here; he has served his purpose and will only slow us down.'

I reached for my blade and Kvist stepped back, fearing my advance.

'Helga no,' screamed Guthrom, but it was too late. I had already pushed my knife into Kvist's throat and pulled it sideways. His windpipe gave some resistance, but my blade was sharp and as his blood gushed over my hand, I spat in his face. Sadly, his death was swift, something he did not deserve.

Guthrom jumped from his horse and grabbed Kvist by the arms, pulling him toward a pile of rocks at the bottom of the cliff.

'Help me cover him up, quickly.'

Cinead joined us as we piled rocks over his corpse hoping to hide him.

'Girl, you're a nightmare. What were you thinking? We don't have time for this?'

I was calm and looked Guthrom straight in the eye before answering.

'I did it for her,' pointing at Manara. 'He took her from her home and made her a slave. Is that not reason enough Guthrom?'

He looked at Manara, and at the moment, I believe he saw the plight of his own daughter written upon her face.

'Maybe you are right,' Guthrom acknowledged.

'It felt right.'

'Let's get moving then. We will make our way to Trondheim; we have friends there.' Guthrom ordered.

'Oddvar won't follow us there,' Cinead replied.

'What's in Trondheim?' I asked.

'Trolls,' joked Erik.

But the joke was short-lived, as riders appeared ahead of us, blocking our path once more.

'Now what do we do?' I cursed.

CHAPTER TWELVE

We watched the horseman drifting slowly towards us
through the valley. Long Shadows crept across the valley floor,
as the sun dipped towards the horizon.

Guthrom counted around fifty men, a small group, probably
a raiding party returning home. They carried shields and wore
battle dress, and Cinead recognized some of the shield designs.

'They're Heggelund's men, might be the ones we saw earlier.'

Guthrom nodded in agreement.

'Maybe we should split up,' Erik suggested.

'No, that would arouse suspicion. Better to act calmly, as if
we're just passing through. There is a split in the valley up
ahead. We will reach it before they do. We can turn West and
head through Gaulardal towards Oppland. If we reach the river
we may be able to sell the horses and pay for passage to

Vingulmark; from there we can travel home.'

'No,' I objected. 'I'm not selling Thunder.' It was a ridiculous statement to make under the circumstances, and I cursed my immaturity.

'I understand. A gift from a father is a precious thing,' Guthrom conceded. 'But there are many horses in this world, and only one of you; I hope.' He smiled gently and for the first time I saw a warmth and humour behind those tired eyes. 'My duty is to get you home in one piece with or without your horse.'

I bit my lip and nodded.

When the Gods are with you, there is no greater feeling. However, when angered, your world feels disjointed and fortune turns sour. Just as we reached the fork in the valley, Oddvar and his men appeared behind us and I wondered if the Gods were angry with me for killing Kvist.

Cinead cursed our luck and Guthrom cursed it further as the war-band also turned west, following us into the valley. We were being herded like sheep to the slaughter, and I feared the Gods had finally abandoned us completely.

The skies were darkening and Oddvar would not yet know that the war-band was composed of Heggalund's men. He was too far away to see their shields in this fading light. Hopefully he would hesitate and wait until morning. The new day however would bring clarity, and he would surely join them and together they would hunt us down.

Tiredness descended with the darkness, but we could not rest. We had to push on putting as much distance between ourselves and our adversaries as we could. So, as the hand of darkness covered the valley floor, we dismounted and continued the journey on foot.

Every step was arduous. There was no moon to guide us, and a clouded sky had extinguished the stars. The valley narrowed and the once gentle slopes turned ever more mountainous and rocky with every step. Erik struggled, his wounds sore from the ride. He needed to rest and was now forced to lean on Manara for support.

'We need to stop Guthrom. Erik can't go on much further.'

'We will rest for a short while, but we need to keep going. I will go back a way and see how far our pursuers are behind us, hopefully they will have made camp for the night. You scout ahead Cinead, we don't want to run into any more surprises.' As Cinead disappeared into the darkness, Guthrom did the same, and a strange silence descended on those of us who remained behind. I removed the balm that Groa had given me and offered it to Erik.

'Rub this onto your wounds. Groa said it would help you heal.' Erik nodded, but Manara grabbed it off him.

'I will do it you lay back and rest,' she whispered.

'With pleasure,' he smirked, and I coughed to remind them I

was still here.

'What did the witch tell you, Helga? And what were you dreaming about?' Erik's sudden enquiry made me feel uncomfortable.

'Oh, nothing important,' I lied. 'I need to learn to trust people more, and she said I would be a magnificent leader.' Erik forgot himself and laughed out loud, but we shushed him as his amusement rattled along the valley walls.

'Quiet, you will get us all killed.' I whispered.

'Yes, my queen,' he mocked, and Manara giggled.

'I wish I hadn't told you now, you will forever mock me.' He smiled and reached for my hand.

'No, I won't Helga. Groa talks to the Gods, I have heard her, and felt their presence. If that is what she said, then believe it, I pray I am around to see it.' He squeezed my hand, then lay back. 'Now let me rest and be tended too by this beautiful woman,' Manara smirked and began applying the balm whilst I walked away to attend to Thunder.

Time passed so slowly, and Erik and Manara were sleeping when Guthrom returned.

'Wake them up, where's Cinead?' he enquired.

'He's not returned yet.'

'Then we leave without him. He must be up ahead somewhere. I'm sure we will run into him.' I heard the concern in his voice, which worried me.

'I'm sure he's fine.'

Guthrom did not reply. He just motioned his head toward the sleeping couple.

I roused Erik with a kick, forgetting all about his injuries. He yelped like a small dog before reaching for his sword and shield.

'What's wrong?' He enquired.

'We're leaving, wake Manara up.' I ordered.

'You see these wounds Helga, they will eventually be scars

and a reminder of the wonderful times we have spent together. I am sure they will not be the last, but if you kick me like that again, for no good reason, you too will have scars, on your arse. Where's Cinead?' he asked gingerly, getting to his feet.

'He's not returned yet.'

'He can look after himself. We will find him, don't worry,' Erik assured me. But I was worried. He should have been back by now, and I feared that something may have happened to him.

We continued our journey on foot and in silence. With every step I expected Cinead to appear, but as slivers of muted light cracked in the eastern sky, I feared for his safety.

'Guthrom?' I asked. 'What kind of place is this Oppland?'

'It's full of thieves, dirty women and fighting men, a bit like Vestfold.' He winked and almost smiled. 'Why do you ask?'

'Cinead.' I patted Thunder to distract my rising emotions.

'I'm certain he's fine Helga, he is not the bumbling fool that people think he is. I have stood with Cinead in a shield wall many times. Trust me, he can look after himself. Thor's hammer may strike fear through the heavens, but it's Cinead's axe that men fear on the ground. He has saved my life several times over the years, and I curse him for it.'

'Why do you curse him, surely he deserves your gratitude? You should be grateful, I would have left you to die.'

Guthrom roared with laughter.

'I'm sure you would have Helga and I would have thanked you for it. There is no honour at being a cripple amongst warriors. It seems you are more of a Viking than Cinead.'

'I have lived in Vestfold for seven summers and still I don't understand your ways. I have watched you fight Guthrom, you are still a warrior, you remind me of Gunnolf.'

'The wolf? Why Because I am old and grey?'.

'Partly yes, but also because like Gunnolf you stalk your

prey, slowly and methodically looking for weaknesses. They think you're frail, but you're not. They think you're a cripple, but you're not, and when they step forward full of swagger and confidence to strike you down, you attack with guile and biting ferocity. They are no match for the grey wolf.'

Guthrom stopped walking. He seemed embarrassed by my words and struggled to find his own.

'It seems I may have misjudged you, child.'

I hated being called that and he knew it, but this time I took no offence.

'There is no greater feeling than standing with men in a shield wall Helga. The smell of fear, excitement, vomit and piss. The crescendo of noise, curses and prayers to the gods, then the hammering swords on the shields, and the blood-lust for battle. Shields raised high, we move together as one. Slowly at first, then with increasing momentum until,' Guthrom clapped his hands, 'like thunder, we clash together and the killing starts.

Pushing and pulling at our enemies, striking where we can, severing tendons, crushing skulls and slitting throats. A rainstorm of crimson; and as the dying fall, we crush and stab at them. Bloodying the earth, leaving corpses trailing behind us. There they remain until the crows have feasted and the Valkyries have collected their souls, carrying them gently to the feasting halls of Odin and Freya.' He paused, sighing before adding. 'Oh, how I miss it.'

'Well, I would stand next to you in a shield wall.' I stated bluntly.

'Then you would probably die and the Gods would lock the gates of Valhalla for their own protection,' His response was amusing and made me laugh. Guthrom was starting to grow on me.

CHAPTER THIRTEEN

The morning was in full voice, as bird song echoed throughout the valley. The sun cracked through the grey clouds, pushing them apart as it caressed my face with its warming glow. Moss and grass, had replaced the uneven stony ground, allowing me to rest my aching legs as Thunder carried me swiftly along at a gentle trot. Erik, with Manara sat behind him, rode alongside me. He winced occasionally, as Cloud threw his head back and fought against the reins. The stallion was more headstrong than Thunder and needed strong handling; either that or he just preferred Manara's feminine touch over Erik's. I had offered to let Eric ride Thunder, but he was reluctant to do so, preferring the feel of Manara's arms around his waist than a more comfortable ride.

Guthrom brought up the rear, anxiously looking back along

the valley. There was no sign of the warriors we had observed the day before, or Oddvar's group; whilst relieved, he wondered why they had not followed us into Gaulardal.

We surged onwards; the valley narrowing, gorse and bracken gave way to trees and grasses, and I breathed a sigh of relief when the valley turned northwards and opened up into a vast vista of forest, as far as my eyes could see.

'Helga,' Guthrom was waving his arm for me to join him.

'What is it?' I asked.

'I want you to go back and scout the valley. Find out why we have not seen anyone since yesterday.'

His request brought a surge of excitement.

'Take no risks,' he said, gesturing towards a rocky outcrop that stuck out high above the valley below.

'Make your way up there, you should have a good viewpoint, make sure you stay out of sight. Take Thunder as far as you can, then climb the rest of the way on foot. Just find out what they are doing and come straight back. I will lead the others northward until we reach that tree line.' He pointed to a clearing, a slight gap in the mass of green.

'We will wait for you there.'

I nodded and smiled, unable to contain myself.

'I expect you back by midday no later.' He paused before adding, 'If only Cinead was here.'

'Then you wouldn't have to send me. But let's be honest, it would take Cinead all day and night to climb up there. Don't worry Guthrom, I will return safely.'

'Make sure you do, now get going and may Thor keep you safe.'

The sun had travelled far by the time I reached the outcrop. The climb had been tough and exhausting. Thunder had hauled me so far, but once the terrain became too steep, I was forced to leave him grazing and traverse the rest of the way on foot. It was so steep in places, that I had to scramble my way on all fours. The climb was arduous, and I had to stop several times recover my breath before continuing.

Upon reaching the top, I laid flat and crawled to the edge of the outcrop, peeking over the raised edge. The view was incredible and I could see far off into the distance. However, I did not need good eyesight to see the thousands of men that were camping near to my vantage point. This was no longer a war-band, it was an army, and I wondered where they might be travelling too. Were they going to follow our route through Gaulardal into Oppland, or maybe they planned to move south towards Vestfold. There was no love lost between my stepfather and Heggalund, and they would need an army of this size to attack my home. We had many allies that would join us to fight against such an aggressor, but an army this size, with more still arriving, would be a force to reckon with. I had to tell Guthrom, and quickly. He would know what to do.

I had taken great care when making the climb and was pretty

certain that no one was aware of my presence, however I had not considered that advanced scouts may find my horse and wonder where its rider was. There were four of them, all well-armed and they were looking in my direction. I crouched low behind a large boulder and considered my options. I knew as soon as I moved, they would spot me. So I figured my best course of action was to wander down towards them and act unconcerned.

Sometimes being a youthful woman has its advantages, and this was one of them. I smiled as I approached and waved a greeting.

'What you doing here, girl?'

I guessed my inquisitor held rank over the other three, as his clothing and weaponry were far superior compared to that of his comrades.

'Oh, I come here all the time. I like it up there. It makes me feel close to the Gods and sometimes I am gifted with eggs from the ground-nesting birds that live there. Sadly, today I have not been blessed. Maybe I have been too wicked or unworthy.' I bit my bottom lip seductively, whilst running a hand through my hair, but ignored my flirtatiousness and continued his questioning.

'This is a fine horse. Have you stolen it? Maybe that is why you are here alone, you're a thief and in hiding, or perhaps there is something more you're not telling us? You will come with us.'

Sometimes when things seem dire and all hope seems lost, the gods throw you a rope.

I grinned. 'The horse is mine and I am not going anywhere with you, I'm far from alone and if I was you, I would leave now.'

I had spotted the approaching horses riding from the west and recognized the colossal figure that led the way. They were still some way off, but Cinead had spotted me and was now making haste towards us. He seemed to have found some friends too, as there were over thirty men with him, more than enough to persuade these four to leave without further address.

'Don't you want to stay and meet my brother,' I mocked as they hurried away towards the gathering army.

Now wanting to waste any more time I leapt upon Thunders back and galloped towards my rescuers.

'Cinead nice of you to show your face at last.' I was so happy to see him and wanted to throw my arms around his neck and hug him tightly, but affection was a personal thing and not one I cared to share with strangers.

'I found Guthrom and the others, he wanted me to make sure you were keeping out of trouble, which, as always, you failed to do.' He sat with his arms crossed over his horse's neck and smirked at me while the others laughed.

'I will gut the next man that laughs at me.' I spat, annoyed at the mockery.

'I told you she had a temper and no sense of humour.'

Cinead looked at the man next to him.

He was young, maybe eighteen summers. His blonde hair hung wild and loose, cascading down to his shoulders. He was taller than me, but not by much. His build suggested he was a warrior, yet he lacked any visible scars. He was dressed in a quality mail that boasted status. He was very handsome, and he knew it. I struggled to avert my gaze as his lips curled into a wide grin. If Thor ever took human form, then this is what he would surely look like, I thought. All that was missing was his hammer.

'Forgive us Helga. Cinead has told me a lot about you, but he failed to mention your outstanding beauty. I am honoured to meet you.'

I knew I looked a mess, covered in dirt from days of riding. My hair was tangled and matted, and I was sure I didn't smell too good, either. I climbed up onto Thunder's back before responding.

'Maybe a proper introduction would be more appropriate than your failed attempt at flattery.' I was not used to receiving such compliments, and his attentions made me feel a little awkward.

'Again my apologies.' He bowed his head graciously before continuing. 'I am Rognvaldr Eysteinsson, son of Eystein Glumra, the Jarl of Oppland you may have heard of him.'

I shook my head. 'No, I have not heard of you or your father, but I hope he has many men, for beyond that rise an army gathers, an enormous army with thousands of men.'

'Thousands?'

'Go look for yourself, Rognvald Eysteinsson, if you doubt my word.' I tapped my heels on Thunder's flanks and rode off without saying another word.

'She has spirit,' I heard Rognvaldr say, but did not quite catch Cinead's response. I imagined it was not as polite.

Guthrom was waiting where he said he would be. It was well

past midday, and the light was starting to fade; so he had chanced lighting a small fire, probably to guide me to his position rather than to keep out the chill of the evening air.

'You're late,' he said, as I climbed off Thunder's back. The warmth of his embrace surprised me, he was relieved to see me, after my delayed return. 'Where's the others?' he asked.

'Not far behind, there is a huge army Guthrom, thousands of men. They are camped just beyond the outcrop. Cinead and his newfound friends wanted to see for themselves. I think they believe I exaggerate the numbers. I'm not Guthrom, and I'm pretty certain these men are not after us. I think Heggalund is there.'

'You saw him?' he enquired.

'No but there are too many of his men present for him not to be.'

Just then, the others appeared, cantering towards us.

'We somehow need to get word to your father.' He remarked,

watching them dismount.

'Has Helga told you?' Cinead asked.

'She has,' he replied. His voice was sharp and cold, and even Cinead seemed shocked by his manner.'I asked you to make sure she was all right, yet she came back on her own. Why is that?' Cinead looked confused and Rognvaldr started to explain, but was abruptly cut off by Guthrom's raised hand. 'Well?' he urged further.

'We wanted to see this army for ourselves, Guthrom.' Cinead said, perturbed by the line of questioning.

'I sent Helga to scout the valley, not you. You weren't here. I asked you to make sure she was safe and to bring her back here, and only that. You have wasted valuable time, Cinead, time we can't afford. Never ever doubt Helga's word again.' He walked away without saying another word before sitting next to Erik and Manara who were enjoying the warmth of the fire.

'Don't feel bad Cinead, I'm not offended by your mistrust.' I was rubbing salt into his wounds and enjoying it. Rognvaldr smirked, enjoying my teasing.

'Don't know why you're finding it amusing,' I snarled. 'Surely you could have escorted me back yourself, whilst Cinead confirmed my findings. Anything could have happened to me.' His smirk quickly diminished.

'Men… you only consider women when your cocks are twitchy, your bellies empty, and when your clothes need repairing, you're all the same.' I walked away, leaving my statement hanging; murmurings followed, but there was no response.

As darkness descended, the first droplets of rain began to fall, attacking the dancing flames that angrily spat back curses, annoyed by the intrusion.

'Get some rest. We will leave at first light,' said Guthrom, placing a caring hand on my shoulder. It had been another gruelling day, but for the first time in my life, I felt useful.

Guthrom had put his trust in me and I had delivered. I felt

proud and had a fresh sense of purpose and belonging.

Heggalund was here, true, a vast army surrounded him, but he

was still close by and I could feel the first pangs of hatred

welling up in my stomach. Where was he going? What was his

plan? So many questions and no answers, I thought.

CHAPTER FOURTEEN

We followed the river north-westerly through Gudbrandsdalen. It was mountainous and arid, a far cry from Vestfold, with its lowland farmlands and coastal shoreline. However, it was beautiful, albeit desolate. I imagined living here would be a constant fight against the elements, let alone any enemies.

Rognvaldr rode with me. He seemed proud of his homeland and talked constantly as we travelled.

'Those mountains are called Smuibelgen,' he said, pointing to a collection of peaks that broke the skyline and disappeared into low-hanging clouds. 'They are often capped with snow, not a place you want to be in the winter months.'

I laughed as I found the name amusing.

'A strange name for a group of mountains,'

'It means blacksmiths bellows, as when the wind blows it gusts through the ranges, hence the name.'

'I like that better than Smeebeggin,' I remarked. He smiled but decided against correcting my mispronunciation.

'Tell me Rognvaldr; how many men can your father raise in battle.' My question seemed to flummox him, and he stuttered before answering.

'I'm not sure, maybe four, five hundred men; our people are scattered throughout the Kingdom. It would take time to send word and gather an army, but have no fear Helga, we can defend ourselves.' My abruptness had ruffled his feathers, I could tell, so I curtailed my tongue and softened my tone.

'I am sure you can, Rognvaldr, but if that army comes this way, I fear your people would fall and your father's kingdom lost. There are three times as many men in Gaulardal and more were arriving. You saw it for yourself, Heggalund has ambition.'

'So does your father.' He surprised me with his sharpness. It was almost venomous. 'My father knows that he wishes to rule as King of all these lands. He is as much as a threat to us as Heggalund is.'

I could not deny what he said. My father did have ambition; he had won many battles and now ruled several districts near Vestfold, and It was true he desired to unite all these lands; yet to achieve this, he also needed support. It was not something he could do on his own. My father was shrewd and realized to succeed, he needed agreeable men around him, people he could trust to manage these districts on his behalf. These fylki's paid taxes to him and swore their allegiance; but in return for their loyalty, they had prospered. Trading had improved and wealth with it. People did not starve as much as they used to, and under my father's rule, they had thrived. Vestfold had become a major trading point, with goods being bought and sold all over the known world. We bought spices and silk, silver and glass and in return sold honey, wheat, iron and furs. Even our trees were sold, and as a child, I often wondered if trees grew anywhere else but here.

Rognvaldr had been friendly to us up to now, but I began to wonder where his fathers' loyalties might lay.

'I would choose your friends carefully. My father is an outstanding leader and warrior, your people would be well advised to have him as an ally rather than an enemy.' I was slightly terse in my reply, but Rognvaldr didn't react. He chose instead to ignore my comment, at least for now.

The rest of our journey comprised only polite conversation. He showed a significant interest in the island of my birth, with its fertile lands and good fishing. I was happy to tell him as much as I could remember about my old home. I quite liked him; not only was he handsome, but he was respectful too. I felt he judged me as an individual and not just as a woman, that to me was his best quality.

He sent two riders ahead to inform the King of our impending arrival, and it surprised me to see that many had gathered to greet us as we rode in.

'Welcome my friends, welcome.' We dismounted and the man who greeted us hugged Rognvaldr warmly. It wasn't hard to guess who this man was, as the likeness to Roganvaldr was striking. 'You must be hungry after your journey. Come inside before the rain comes.' He smiled, but I felt his unease and Cinead noticed it too.

'He's worried,' whispered Cinead.

'So would I be in his shoes,' agreed Guthrom. 'He knows he can't defend himself against Heggalund, and he fears Harald may also have an eye on his Kingdom.'

'Will father take his Kingdom?' I asked, which made Guthrom laugh.

'He will at some point, by treaty or by force and that will depend on its King.'

I could not understand why men would fight and die over land that was so arid, desolate and wild. Surely it would be better to fight for somewhere more fertile, rich and yielding. To me that made more sense.

Eystein Glumra sat at the head of the table in the main hall. Hundorp was a large settlement cradled into the belly of a rolling hillside that overlooked the Gudbrandsdalslagen, a river of ample proportions, good fishing and trade routes. Maybe this was a place worth fighting for after all.

Aseda, his wife, sat next to him. She was unusually tall and elegant, very slim with long black hair, which was yet to show the flecks of age. She was obviously younger than her husband and sat silently, nibbling at a succulent trout that graced her plate.

She kept looking at me, which unnerved me slightly; maybe it was because Rognvaldr had sat beside me. I smiled whilst tearing my fish apart unceremoniously, throwing the head to the waiting hounds that sat beside our hosts.

'Does your mother ever smile?' I asked jokingly.

'She's not my mother. My actual mother died in childbirth,' he replied.

'Oh, I'm sorry, I didn't mean to offend.' He held up his hand.

'It's fine Helga, Aseda has looked after my brother and I well. My father adores her and relies on her council. She has a clever head on her shoulders; don't underestimate her Helga. My father does very little without her approval.'

'Guthrom, tell me all about this army.'

'Ask Helga, my Lord, she is the one who saw it first.' I glared at him as he poured himself an ale. I hesitated, but the hall fell silent in anticipation of what I was about to say.

'My lord,' I stuttered. 'The army is vast, over a thousand strong and growing.'

The gasps and mummers passed around the hall and I waited

for them to fall silent.

'She is a woman they exaggerate.' A man shouted.

'Who's that Rognvaldr?' I asked.

'That is my brother Sigurd,' he replied.

'I think you will find my lord. It is men that exaggerate the size of things and women that feel the truth of it.' I smiled whilst taking my thumb and forefinger and reducing the gap between them until it was the size of an acorn. The Hall shuddered with laughter, and even Aseda grinned acknowledgment at my sarcastic response.

'I have seen them also father Helga speaks the truth.' I nodded at Rognvaldr, appreciating his support.

'Go and look for yourself, they are not hiding, they have no need to.' I let my words sink in before resuming.

'They came from the north and the east and were still arriving when I left. Shields of many designs and colours, most of which I do not know. However, one design I did recognise, and that belongs to Jarl Heggalund.'

A hush descended like a mournful fog. There were no more interruptions, as the mere mention of Heggalund was enough to silence the room. Sigurd looked at me, but said nothing.

'My Lord, if I might suggest,' Guthrom gestured. The king did not respond verbally, but nodded a reply.

'If this army marches west through Gaulardal, you will lose your kingdom. I suggest you send a messenger to Vestfold and ask Harald Harfagre for his support.'

The hall almost imploded at the suggestion. Screams of *'never'* and *'we will fight alone,'* bombarded our table. Men and women pushed towards Guthrom, their actions and spitting insults causing Erik and Cinead to rise together and reach for their swords. Guthrom raised a hand to stop them as I sat motionless, devouring yet another one of the glorious fish that lay in front of me.

'Enough,' the King yelled. 'Let him speak.'

Order was restored apart from the odd muttering that seemed amplified above the quiet. The King's glare was enough to silence those individuals.

'Guthrom, forgive their exuberance, please continue.' Guthrom gave a shallow bow of gratitude. I now realized why my father held him in such high esteem and kept him in a position of power. I had seen him fight, but now I saw a different side to Guthrom, his skills at diplomacy.

'My Lord, I meant no offense, but my King could be of substantial support to your people in these times. You cannot fight this army alone, and even with Harald's help there is no certainty of victory.'

Eystein sat thoughtfully, but it was his son Sigurd that responded first.

'Maybe we should ally with Heggelund and march south on Vestfold. Harald would be defeated against such numbers, and we would save Hundorp.' He smirked and followed up with,

'An army of ample proportions, wouldn't you agree?' I looked up from my meal and our eyes met, but I resisted a response. He had made his point, but the added remark was an unnecessary addition and made him look petty.

'Do it,' I said calmly. 'Join Heggalund if you so desire. I'm sure he would welcome you with open arms; but don't presume Vestfold would fall. My father has many warriors at his disposal and has won many victories. You think you can trust Jarl Heggalund? He will deceive you with his false promises and then take your kingdom as his own. Your woman will be raped and your children enslaved, they will bring only slaughter to those who resist. I have seen his work with my own eyes. Ask Cinead, he will tell you.' I continued eating, then added. 'Your fish are delicious, truly a gift from the Gods.'

Everyone in the hall stared at me as I pulled a fish bone from my pursed lips and flicked it across the table.

With the room now quiet, Guthrom spoke once more.

'You have a tough decision to make, King Glumra, not one I would like to make myself, and it is true King Harald wants to be king of all these lands. However, one man can't rule a country alone. He rewards his allies well, and many prosper from his kindness, as could you if you were to support him.' Allowing Eystein to digest his words, he continued. 'He will be well aware of the army that masses on your border and will raise an opposing force himself, of that I am certain. He will wonder where your allegiance lies my Lord, and won't take it for granted that he has your support. Trust me, he is a ruthless adversary when riled and Odin's Hall has benefitted the most from his victories.'

It was a gentle threat but a threat never the less and I watched as Glumra refilled his drinking horn and raised it to his lips. He downed the ale, then walked away from the table, Aseda obediently following. Before disappearing into his quarters, he muttered:

'You will have my decision in the morning, Guthrom.'

With the king retiring to his bedchamber, others dispersed

too. Rognvaldr remained seated next to me as his brother quickly exited, grabbing a slave girl as he passed. She squealed and protested, but his back-handed slap silenced her into submission.

'Your brother seems to favour an alliance with Heggalund. What about you, Rognvald?' This was the first time Cinead had spoken, favouring the ale rather than the conversation.

'My brother is a warrior with little interest or knowledge in politics. I think he probably sees Heggalund as more like himself, so believes that his own warrior status maybe enough to protect the throne. Like you, however, I do not believe this to be true. I have heard the rumours of the Jarl's cruelty and butchery, and fear he cannot be trusted.'

'It's not a rumour,' Cinead remarked.

'Maybe so, but I must honour my father's decision, whatever that may be.'

Cinead downed another helping of ale, then left the table

without further utterance. The rest of us followed him outside; it had been a tiresome day, and I longed to return home; but destiny had brought me here to Hundorp, and I wondered if I would ever see Vestfold again.

CHAPTER FIFTEEN

The village was silent, apart from the sound of boats knocking together in the gently flowing river. The stars blinked in a cloudless night sky, as I walked along the riverbank with Rognvaldr.

'Tell me, don't you have an opinion of your own? Or do you always hide in the shadow of your father and brother?' My words stung, as I knew they would, but I needed to know whether I could trust him. I liked him and I knew he liked me. I had little to no experience of matters of the heart but his reluctance to leave my side and the constant glances suggested he was interested and wanted more than friendship. I knew he loved this land and its people, and I couldn't help thinking if he were King, he would give up everything to protect it. He responded just as I had expected:

'This is my home, Helga. I would gladly fight and die to protect it. I believed Guthrom when he said that Harald would reward our loyalty if allied; but my father is my King and so I will follow his lead, even if that means fighting for Heggalund.'

'You are right to honour your father, but I hope and pray to Thor that you will fight with me and not against me. Heggalund is a monster, and if we are all to prevail and halt his tyranny, then we will need every sword and shield we can muster to stand against him.' I stopped walking and looked across the river. It was so peaceful and serene.

'You're not like any other woman I have ever met,' Rognvaldr whispered. 'You talk of war and battle the need for revenge; you should be careful Helga; it may get you killed.' He seemed genuinely concerned, which pleased me and so I turned and faced him.

'If I'm to die, fighting alongside people I love and care about, then so be it. If the Gods decide my time here is over, then hopefully I will die with a sword in my hand, not a needle and thread. All I need is someone to teach me the skills of a warrior. I hate it when I'm told it's not my place. Women fight every day. We fight to be seen, to be heard, to give birth. Our strength and fighting spirit are only matched by the Gods themselves, and you men are weak in comparison.' Rognvaldr smirked, which riled me.

'I hate that look, so wipe it from your face. All men have such long noses,' I cursed.

'What is that supposed to mean,' he asked, raising his eyebrows.

'It's the way you look down them at us woman folk, I hate it. Now go away and leave me alone.'

'Helga,' he pleaded. 'Why are you being like this? Not all men are as you say.' I turned on him and he took a step back, convinced I was crazed enough to attack him.

'Will you teach me then?' I glared at him, daring him to

answer.

'No, I won't.' He was calm and spoke softly, but I was like an angry dragon, whose fiery breath wanted to engulf him and turn him into ash. Then, he kissed me, and as fast as my anger had risen, the calming waters of self-control and shock washed over me, my petulance subsiding.

We sat for a while in silence, neither knowing what to say next. I gazed at the moon-touched ripples that danced across the river's surface, and remembered my mother's voice that had been so clear to me in that dark, cold, foreboding sea. She had told me to live, to fight and survive, and here I was all these summers later. I wrapped my arms around my legs, noticing the chill.

'I'm sorry Rognvaldr, you're right I am not like other women. Guthrom calls me wild and untamed, and I think he is probably right. I lack control, clarity of thought, and most of all I tend to put my own needs before others, regardless of the danger.'

Despair engulfed me. One moment I was angry, the next sad, all without tears. I was like a storm cloud without the rain. I felt bereft, confused, and wished my mother was still alive to help me, as only a mother could.

Rognvaldr placed a hand on my cheek. I turned to face him and he pushed my red hair to one side, cradling my neck as he pulled me towards him. Our lips met again and my mouth opened to accept his lustful tongue.

Nakedness is ill advised in such cold climates. It causes more bumps and hollows upon the body than there was in the valley and fields of this wind-swept country. Yet to say my field was well ploughed would be a fair statement, and I purred in satisfaction as I crept into the outbuilding where the others were sleeping peacefully, or so I thought.

'Who taught you that lesson?' Guthrom grunted. I jumped like a naughty child caught in an act of disobedience.

'What are you talking about?' I asked innocently.

Guthrom sat up.

'Using your womanly charms to get what you want. I am old and wise enough now to understand the devious ways of women, Helga. Your sorcery, weaving your spells, manipulating, until we succumb to your will, weakened by your magical powers.' He put his hand to his head and gasped as if ill.

'Your words dribble from your arse, Guthrom. Too much ale has puddled your brain.' I settled onto the straw-covered floor, picking a hand full up and sniffing it before throwing it in his direction. 'Smell it, your shit is everywhere.' We both laughed, then he winked and smiled warmly.

'Well, at least he's one that won't fight against you in a shield wall.'

'He won't help me fix a sail either, or brush a floor, or teach me to fight.'

Guthrom sighed, then shocked me.

'I will teach you to fight, if that is truly what you want.'

I sat bolt upright and stared at the man who had made my life so difficult since my arrival at Vestfold.

'You will? Why would you do that? After everything you have said about me.'

'I have watched you grow from a child into a woman.' He nonchalantly flicked a hand towards me. 'You're so….' He hesitated, grasping for the right word.

'Annoying?' I grinned.

'Yes, that too, but so many other things as well. I have an extensive list.'

I could tell he felt uncomfortable, this was not a man to talk openly in such a way.

'I hated you growing up,' I said earnestly. 'You were always so bitter and hate filled towards me. All you did was point out my faults, my wild nature, my arrogance, always the bad, you never saw the good.'

'That's because there wasn't any,' he joked. 'Harald told me you were special, a gift from Odin. He told me you would make a great queen one day.'

'Queen? Fuck that.' I grimaced at the thought.

'His words, not mine.' He kicked open the door and I could see the morning light chasing away the night sky.

'You are not that child anymore. I have seen your love, passion and self-belief, your trust and kindness, even with me, and that deserves respect. So I will give you what you want and teach you to fight on one condition.' He looked directly at me.

'What's that?' I asked.

'That you help me find my daughter.'

There were tears in his eyes and he fought hard to contain them.

'I will Guthrom, I promise, but first we must deal with Heggelund.' He nodded and picked up his sword.

'Come on then, grab Cinead's sword, it's time for your first lesson.'

'Now?' I complained. 'I've had no sleep.'

'Exactly, you need to be able to fight even when exhausted, now move.'

CHAPTER SIXTEEN

The sound of steel hitting steel, had drawn a small crowd of bleary-eyed and ale fatigued individuals. Cinead was chomping down on a smoked mackerel and what looked like half a loaf of bread. Erik shouted curses at me and mocked my technique, whilst Manara squealed with excitement and encouragement. It was still just the basics, but I was revelling in it. Thrusting and parrying, attacking and defending, my arm ached, but I didn't care. I just wanted it to go on forever.

Rognvaldr appeared, which caught my eye and distracted me. Guthrom stepped forward quickly, parrying my hesitant blow. His elbow connected with my head, which hurt like hell and sent me flying backwards, arms flailing. I fell arse first onto the damp, muddy ground. I could see everyone laughing, but the ringing in my ears deprived me of their taunts and jests. Guthrom reached down and pulled me to my feet.

'Look away on the battlefield and your head will follow your eyesight to Valhalla,' he whispered. It was a lesson well taught and not one I would repeat.

'That's enough for now. We will resume again when there are fewer distractions.' He gestured towards Rognvaldr, raising his eyebrows and mimicking a kiss.

'One day I will put you on your arse Guthrom and everyone will laugh at you.' It was a humorous threat, but I meant it and knew one day I would make it happen. My mentor just laughed and turned to walk away, so I punched him in on the back of his head as hard as I could.

'Never turn your back on an enemy,' I whispered as he spun round to face me. I smirked as he stared.

'You will pay for that girl, but not today.'

I kissed his check and laughed at his discomfort. Guthrom had somehow created a place in my heart which I had never thought was possible, and I wondered where our new friendship would take us both.

'Only a cripple would allow a girl to hit him like that,' a voice boomed from behind the crowd. It parted, and Sigurd strolled through the throng.

Guthrom ignored the jibe, but I did not.

'For the son of a King you lack respect,' I spat as Guthrom grabbed my arm.

'Leave it Helga, we need these people with us, not against us.'

'You should listen to your cripple friend, and as for respect I save that for those who fight with men, not woman.'

'Sigurd, that's enough,' said Rognvaldr forcefully, as he moved towards me. He could see that I was angry and feared I would react, which I was really tempted to do.

'Ahh, little brother, you have boned her, haven't you? Good for you, that is all the bitch is worth. I hope she didn't charge you too much.'

Insulted, I moved to step forward, but Rognvaldr stepped in front of me.

'No Helga, I will deal with this.' He glared at me and I saw the anger whirling in the pools of his eyes.

'You go too far, brother,' he spat, and removed his sword from its scabbard.

'You dare to raise your sword to me, Rognvaldr, over that.' He pointed a gnarly finger at me, and I sneered back.

'I can't believe you would fight me over an insignificant piece of meat like her. How sad.' He removed his own sword as one villager passed both brother's matching shields.

'Stop this,' I screamed and everyone looked at me.

'Sigurd, you offend my eyes and if you truly want to fight, then fight me. Not with sword and shield, but hand to hand.' He roared with amusement, as did some villagers, but the people who knew me well stood rigid, their faces expressionless.

'You're calling me out, Helga? I am a warrior I have faced and killed many men in battle. I do not need to prove myself against a mere woman. I will hump you, but I will not fight you.' He laughed again, as did the crowd.

'Argr,' I spat, and his laughter ceased. Throwing down his sword and shield, he removed the jacket and shirt. Calling him unmanly had worked like a charm.

'So be it,' he conceded. 'Give me room this won't take long.'

Everyone stepped back as Guthrom put a hand on my shoulder.

'Helga, you know you're insane, don't you? Walk away now and I will smooth things over with Sigurd.'

'No, I'm sick of everyone looking after me, protecting me, thinking me weak. I will kick that bastard's arse.'
Guthrom shook his head.

'If you die Harald will kill me too, you know that don't you.'

'I had better live then.' I said, turning to see Sigurd standing like a mountain. He now seemed so much bigger than before. His hair fell into a tangled mass, merging with his grubby beard. His now bare chest rippled with well-defined muscle and was covered in battle scars and tattoos. This will hurt, I thought. The crowd was multiplying, and Rognvaldr pleaded with me to stop. I pushed him forcefully away and stood my ground.

'He limps slightly on his left side, so make him turn that way it will give you an advantage, albeit a small one.' Erik whispered in my ear, whilst pulling my red hair back and tying it tight into a ponytail.

'I had noticed,' I said, 'you taught me well.'

'Don't get hit too much,' he whispered.

'If I die, I expect revenge,' I looked at him and he smiled.

'Of course, count on it.'

Sigurd strolled in, expecting to give me two slaps and put me straight down. That was his first mistake. His flailing fist was easily avoided and brushed past me as I leaned away. If it had connected, I would have probably never recovered, but because of his arrogance, he lacked control and missed. However, I did not. With a double-handed fist, I aimed for his neck, but unfortunately, hit his bulging shoulder muscles instead. He staggered but remained on his feet. The crowd cheered as Sigurd regained his composure.

'You're quick like a slippery eel, but you can't avoid me forever, my net awaits.' He sped forward again but was more cautious than last time and as I sidestepped to the right he blocked my blow, following up with a right hand of his own that glanced at my cheek, grazing it in the process. It stung but was a glancing blow, and I recovered swiftly enough. He raised his hands and gestured me forward, but I waited patiently, knowing he couldn't resist. This time, as he surged forward, I did the same. Like one of Freya's cats, I leapt forward and dropping to my knees and hit him twice, left then right as hard as I could and straight into his groin. He didn't drop straight away, but as he staggered, I grabbed his weak leg by the ankle and pulled it as hard as I could. The mountain toppled. Struggling to breathe, and holding his manhood, he rolled backwards into the dirt. I leapt to my feet and, jumping high in the air, I stamped on his face. The sound of cracking bone made the crowd groan as his blood burst forth, speckling his face and neck. I had shattered his nose and probably his cheek and several of his blood covered teeth laid next to his split lips. He gurgled on the verge of unconsciousness; but I hadn't finished yet. The lust of battle intoxicated me. It raced through my veins and nourished me. I felt like a goddess. Reaching down my leg, I removed my dagger, planning to plunge it into his chest. I wanted to split skin and muscle and cut out his heart. I yearned to take it in my hands and squeeze it tight until it popped. However, I was denied.

Cinead ploughed into me like a charging bull, knocking me sideways, expelling the air from my lungs as we collided. It hurt to breathe, but I forced myself to my feet and tried to speak.

'Cinead,' I gasped.

'You have won. There is no need to go further,' he spoke gently, but I was raging.

'You deny me?'

'Yes I do, you have restored your honour now let it be Helga.' I was slowly regaining my self-control, my lust retreating as I watched Sigurd being helped to his feet and led away.

'He was right. It didn't take long. He won't forget that in a hurry,' said Erik as he undid my ponytail.

'That might be a problem,' Guthrom added. 'He has been embarrassed, and a wounded wolf is dangerous.'

'You should have let me finish him then.' I quipped.

They all ignored me, including Rognvaldr, who stared at me wide eyed. I had been so tender and loving during our lovemaking; yet now here I was, thirsting for blood and high with battle fever. I was uncertain he liked what he saw.

As we walked together towards the King's hall, several riders arrived from the North, their urgency apparent.

'What is it?' asked Rognvaldr.

'Riders are coming through the valley towards us, my lord. I would say around two hundred warriors. They have a woman and child with them.'

'What did the woman look like?' Guthrom asked.

'She was dressed in grey with a hood, the girl rode with her.'

'Groa and Hella.' I said.

'The witch?' Rognvaldr was surprised. 'Why would she come here?'

'I doubt it's through choice. I need to speak with your father at once,' said Guthrom.

CHAPTER SEVENTEEN

The King was not best pleased to see us so early. We had interrupted him, and as he emerged, I glimpsed Åseda, bare-breasted and flushed.

'What's so urgent that you raise me from my bed so early.'

'Forgive me, father, but riders approach around two hundred of them.'

'You have mustered a welcoming party, I presume?'
Rognvaldr nodded a reply.

'My Lord, I believe they come for us,' explained Guthrom.

'It seems all you have brought me are unwanted problems, Guthrom. First an army on my doorstep and now this, what do they want with you?'

As Guthrom explained, Åseda appeared, now fully dressed.

As she approached me, putting an arm round my shoulder,

she asked if I could plait her hair whilst leading me to a quieter corner within the grand hall.

'I hope my son's performance was pleasurable for you, Helga. He is rather inexperienced compared to Sigurd.' Her statement made me fumble for a response and I wondered how she knew of our dalliance.

'Yes, my lady, he was… fine.'

'I'm glad. Rognvaldr is so very different from his older brother. He is intelligent, thoughtful and like Odin has a lust for knowledge, Sigurd on the other hand has far less between his ears.'

It seemed nothing went unnoticed within Hundrop, so I figured I might as well tell the Queen about my altercation with Sigurd rather than her finding out later from some other source.

It seemed to amuse her that a mere girl could best her battle-hardened son in a fight.

'Well Helga, seems you have made an impression on both my

son's.' I finished her hair and sat awkwardly, not knowing what to say next. After a prolonged silence she asked:

'How's my sister?' I was perplexed.

'Your sister?' I asked.

'Asa... Oh, you didn't know I'm sorry I presumed the others would have told you. Asa is my sister.'

As I stared at her, it became glaringly obvious. Apart from the different hair colour, their features were so similar.

'I see it now,' I remarked. 'You look alike.'

'I will take that as a compliment, thank you, but alas she has nicer hair than I, as do you it seems.'

'It can be troublesome and weighs heavily upon my head. I'm sometimes tempted to cut it short.' I said, making small talk. 'Asa is well, she has been very good to me, even though I test her patience.'

'That's what children are for,' she grinned.

Just then, Sigurd and four others burst into the hall. His face was badly swollen and blood still oozed from his shattered nose and lips. He spoke, but his mouth barely moved and his words were hardly audible.

'What in Hel's name happened to you?' Eystein asked.

Sigurd didn't answer, but glanced in my direction.

Åseda stood and walked towards him.

'It seems our son has injured himself. Too much ale maybe? Or was it something else?' Sigurd looked at his mother and knew she was teasing him. He refrained from answering. 'There is a rider here, he seeks council.' He muttered, dabbing his lip with his sleeve.

'One of Heggalund's men I take it,'

'No father, one of Harald Harfagre's men. He is alone.' Sigurd spluttered.

'Send him in, then tend to the mess that is your face.' Eystein looked at Åseda and her smirk told him she knew what had happened to their eldest son.

When Leif Arneson saw me standing with the others, his sigh of relief was almost tangible. He looked exhausted, but beamed as he approached.

'I've been looking for you for days. I feared you were all dead.'

'Where is my father?' I asked.

'He travels north and gathering men as he goes. We are massing a large army, but it is the size of a sparrow compared to the one that skulks in Gaulardal.'

'I believe you wished to speak to me, or is your reunion more urgent than your message.' Eystein was terse and irritated, which was understandable under the circumstances. He was under threat, with enemies advancing from all directions.

'Forgive me, my Lord,' Leif bowed graciously and continued. 'King Harald sends a message. He requests you join him and his allies to eradicate the threat that gathers in the east. Although their numbers are vast, he is confident that together we can be victorious he is counting on your support.'

The King was churlish in his response.

'Victory or defeat, I will still lose my kingdom. Either Harald or Heggalund will take it from me as they have done to others. Both are a threat to me and I can't fight either of them alone.'

'My Lord, Harald is not threatening your Kingdom,' Guthrom stated.

'Not yet, but he will.' Eystein was agitated, and I felt some sympathy for his plight.

Leif took a step forward…

'My King wants your allegiance, not your land Lord. He wants you to stand with him in the shield wall and not against him. I am to tell you if Heggalund advances on Hundrop, he will help defend it.' Eystein snorted a response. Weighed down by indecision and burden, he slumped onto his throne. Åseda joined him, placing her hand on his.

'Husband,' she said. 'Hundrop has thrived under your governance and we have much to lose. We should fight to preserve what we have, but we can't do it alone. My sister is his queen; we have a family connection. According to Helga and Guthrom, he is an honourable man who keeps his word. Can the same be said of Heggalund? Maybe Harald will let us keep what we have if we stand with him. We can but hope, but we are in no position to defeat both and I personally would rather side with my sister's husband than any other.' The King looked at his Queen fondly. Regardless of the age difference, I could see the love they shared.

'Rognvaldr, what do you say?' The question surprised his son, and he looked at his mother for guidance. She offered none, so I elbowed him gently.

'Answer your father.' I suggested forcefully. He looked at me and I smiled, knowing he would never fight against me. He had proven that against his brother. Guthrom was right. I had forged an alliance whether Rognvaldr wanted it or not.

'I believe we should fight father and I would rather fight with these people than fight for Heggalund. There has been no threat to us until now and it's come from the East, not from the South. If Harald has offered shields, then we should do the same.'

The Queen looked at me and smiled. Men might wield power, I thought, but it's women that control it.

'Very well. How long before Harald arrives?' He asked.

'Four days, maybe five my Lord,' Eystein seemed disappointed, knowing that Hundrop could be overwhelmed by them. As if reading his thoughts, Åseda made a suggestion.

'Hladir is a days ride away. Send word to my father he could get here before Harald,' the King considered her suggestion.

'It would take him three days at most to get here with his men in tow. It may still be too late and our joint forces would still be inadequate. We would still need Harfagre.'

'Maybe there is a way to delay Heggalund.' I muttered.

My idea was risky, and it had more holes than a fisherman's net, but we needed the time and I hoped the riders that approached from Gaulardal might just give us that time.

CHAPTER EIGHTEEN

Greed is the greatest weakness amongst men. Their constant need for wealth, power and land drives them to destruction. Women yearn for a place to call home, somewhere safe to raise their children, a place of quiet and sanctuary. I hoped that the predispositions of men would allow the clouds to pass, the sun to bow and the moon to mock at their cupidity. I requested two days from Odin and hoped it would be enough.

As we watched Oddvar and his warriors approach, I noticed that some of Heggalund's men had joined his ranks. I looked for Groa and Hella, but there was no sign of them, and I wondered why.

Eystein ordered his men to form a shield wall. Three hundred men were squeezed together, shields overlapping and spears protruding like a hedgehog's spikes. It was a formidable sight, and the hairs on my neck bristled with excitement. Another fifty with bows had arranged themselves neatly behind the Skjaldborg. Sigurd and Rognvaldr were imbedded within the throng and shouted encouragement to their comrades. The noise of swords hammering shields thundered across the valley, and I looked skyward, hoping that Thor would add his thunder to ours. But the sky was clear, the sun vibrant, and the black crows mocked me as they swarmed above my head.

Hundrop was easily defended, surrounded mostly by the river, it nestled neatly within its water filled womb. There was only one actual place to attack, and that was well fortified with deep ditches and a palisade. Eystein's shield wall was a show of force no more, for we knew Oddvar was not here to launch an attack. He was here for those who had killed his brother and to deliver a message.

You could see the family resemblance as Oddvar dropped from his horse. He was younger and maybe slightly taller than

Gudlaug had been, but his features mimicked his older brother, and his swagger and gait oozed confidence as he approached the wall.

'Is this how you greet all your guests, Glumra?'

His lack of respect did not impact on Eystein as he stepped through the shield wall accompanied by his two sons.

'This is how I greet guests who arrive with over two hundred well-armed men, yes. I take it you are one of Heggalund's men?' Oddvar smiled, then saw Manara standing close to Erik.

'I see you have my slave; she was meant for Jarl Heggalund and he's very unhappy that she has been taken. It would be a nice gesture if you were to give her back to me.' Eystein glanced at Manara, and for a moment I thought he was considering it.

'I find it hard to believe that the Jarl would gather such an enormous army just to retrieve a slave. I'm happy to give payment to you for her if you wish it, but she stays here with us. She has made some friends, and is no longer a slave.' Oddvar stared coldly towards us and pointed in our direction.

'Her friends killed my brother and a good friend of mine. It is they who should pay. `Maybe with their lives.'

'Ahh, so you are Oddvar the slave trader. It all makes sense to me now. Tell me, how would you like to trade? And what would it take to keep Jarl Heggalund away from my door.'

I could see the confusion, the uncertainty on Oddvar's face, and admired how Eystein was playing his part.

The slaver glanced in our direction once more and must have noticed that we were unarmed and surrounded by a small group of warriors.

'I don't understand, Lord,' he confessed.

'I'm glad that you now deem to address me correctly. This land is my land and I wish to keep it, so I have a proposition for you and your Jarl.' Oddvar said nothing but listened intently.

'I have Harald Harfagre's daughter and I will give her up, if the Jarl gives assurances that my Kingdom will be left out of any conflict with him now, or in the future. She would be a valuable asset to Heggalund; I'm sure Harald would be eager for her safe return. I believe he is very fond of her, but for the life of me, I can't understand why. Still, she would be an excellent bargaining tool, don't you think?' Eystein clasped his hands in front of him and waited for a reply.

I did not believe Oddvar to be a fool or dim-witted, but at that moment he seemed almost childlike. His confidence dissipated like a morning mist, and his lack of immediate response gave me hope. Moments passed before he finally answered.

'It is an interesting offer, but to be honest, we could just come here and take her by force, couldn't we?' His words may have been threatening, but his eyes betrayed him. If you are going to make threats, then you should look at the person you are threatening and not at your own feet. When he did raise his eyes, he was met with an icy glare.

'You threaten me, Oddvar?' Eystein growled, prickled by the arrogant trader who shuffled uncomfortably and once more lowered his gaze.

'No Lord, but let's be truthful, you are in no position to bargain. However, I'm sure it would delight Jarl Heggalund to receive such a gift, along with your allegiance.' This time Oddvar looked directly at the King, eye to eye.

'I am confused, Oddvar. Where do you sit? Do you have a throne? Do you lead an army?' Eystein began pacing around whilst talking, his arms gesturing and mocking. 'Are you King Oddvar?'

'No lord, I'm not a King.' His voice cracked slightly as some of Eystein's men sniggered.

'Then if you have no status, you must be a mere underling and so unworthy of conversation about such important matters, wouldn't you agree?'

Oddvar didn't answer at first. I could tell he was angry and humiliated, but he had been left with no option now but to take the King's offer to Heggalund.

'I will speak to Jarl Heggalund and return the day after tomorrow with his reply, or he may decide to pay you a visit personally.' It was his last attempt to save face, and it made Eystein smile.

'I will roast a pig, tell him.'

Oddvar bowed slightly and mounted his horse. He returned to his men, and we watched as they left. The Gods had been kind they had granted us two more days.

CHAPTER NINETEEN

As soon as Oddvar was out of sight, Leif mounted a fresh horse and left with six men for Hladir. Åseda gave him a gift for her father. It was a simple wooden horse, worn with age, but she told Leif that it was precious and he was not to misplace it. As soon as Hakon Grjotgardsson saw it, he would come, she had told me, and I believed her, for daughters are precious in a father's heart and Hakon had two, both of them were in danger.

'Well, I. guess now we just wait,' Erik said. He was standing with Manara, he had hardly left her side since Groa's cave.

'We need to leave, now.' I stated. Guthrom and Cinead looked at me, then at each other.

'Leave?' Asked Guthrom. 'And go where?'

'We need to find Groa and Hella.'

Guthrom shook his head, as Erik laughed. As for Cinead, he just looked at me as he always did, with total disbelief.

'Don't worry, I have a plan. We need to find Rognvaldr, then I will explain.'

Fairhair always told me I was a devious child, but now, as a youthful woman, I believed I was more calculating and surreptitious than devious. We found Rognvaldr with his mother in the main hall, the Queen beckoned me to sit beside her at the feasting table, it seemed I had made an impression. Eystein had left with Sigurd to raise more men from surrounding villages and wasn't expected back till nightfall.

'I need your help,' I said to Rognvaldr, our eyes meeting like they had the night before. I smiled, but it was not returned.

'Hmm, that surprises me, you didn't seem to need it earlier,' he mumbled. I guess he felt hurt that I did not need his help or protection from Sigurd. I ignored his sourness and continued.

'Then it should be easy for you to betray me,' I said, sneering at his puerility.

Everyone sat quietly as I explained my idea. I believed it

would work, but was uncertain how to implement it. I needed the help of the others, but figured if successful, we could rescue Groa and Hella and give us even more time than the Gods had already kindly permitted.

'There is a derelict farm north of here, it's nestled beyond the valley, not far from where you waited for us Guthrom. Trees surround it, a good place for men to hide, especially under darkness. If we could lure them there, Helga's plan might just work, but it's not without risk.' Rognvaldr's worries were well founded. He knew if anything went wrong, I could well end up in the hands of Heggalund or worse still, we could all end up in Valhalla.

Guthrom looked thoughtful as he stroked his wiry beard and pursed his lips.

'You're not really considering this, are you?' asked Cinead.

'Heggalund might wonder where Oddvar was and wait for his return. It would leave him wondering whether he has an ally here or not, the indecision may cause him to pause and be cautious, that would be to our advantage. We know Harald approaches from the south. Grjotgardsson will hopefully come from the north. If we can persuade Heggalund to come west through Gaulardal when we want him too, then we could trap him in the valley, fight him where it narrows. With our combined forces, we may make a decent fight of it.'

'What if Harald doesn't get here in time?' Cinead challenged.

'Then it won't matter, we will all be dead, anyway.'

I was sure that greed and opportunity would be too big of a lure for Oddvar to resist. After all, he was a trader of woman and children and a King's daughter would surely be too tempting a morsel to ignore. He would profit enormously by delivering me to Heggalund personally, rather than let Eystein use me as a mere bargaining chip.

'We should tell the King,' Rognvaldr stated.

'There is no time to wait, the Queen can tell him on his return.' I knew the King would not be pleased at us changing the plan in his absence, but it was an opportunity that I believed we could not let pass and Guthrom also saw its merit and admired my strategy.

I admit I was nervous when we left Hundorp, but with just over one hundred and fifty men in tow, I was confident that we could defeat Oddvar and his warriors, as long as everything fell into place. If it went awry, then my life would either be lost or changed again forever. Rognvaldr rode next to me, and I could tell he was uneasy.

'I don't like this Helga,' he finally professed.

'It will be fine, trust me.'

Guthrom joined us, his grin removing years from his aged face.

'What are you smiling about?' I asked.

'I could spend half a day explaining it to you, but you still wouldn't understand.' He was wrong. I understood completely.

He felt alive again, no longer the cripple. The chance to be a

warrior again thrilled him, and if he died tonight, he would go

to Odin with that same stupid grin on his face.

'Make me a promise,' he uttered. I turned to face him.

'What's that,' I enquired.

'You mustn't kill Oddvar, no matter what. You know that,

don't you?'

He feared that I would lose control again and kill Oddvar like I

did Kvist. However, if we were to succeed, Oddvar had to live

and, as disappointing as that was, I knew it to be true.

'I won't, I promise, not yet anyway.' Guthrom nodded,

grinning again, as he returned to the others, who followed

closely behind.

Looking back, Erik caught my eye. I had urged him and

Manara to stay behind, but they had refused. Erik's wounds

were healing well, but I believed he was still far from being fit enough for a battle. Yet he said he was feeling good and if there was to be a fight, then there was no way he was going to miss out on that, and where Erik went, Manara followed.

I could see why Erik was smitten. Manara was beautiful. Her long ebony hair hung wildly, framing her elegant face and complementing the colour of her middle-eastern skin. She carried a bow and had a quiver of arrows hanging around her shoulder. There was a lot to like about Manara and although I had only known her a short time, I felt there was a bond between us. I was unaware that she was skilled with a bow, but if her use of it was as good as her riding, then she may be a useful addition to our war-band.

As night approached, so did the rain, accompanied by an icy wind that pained my ears. The clouds seemed depressingly low and their ominous shades reflected my sombre mood. There was no reason for my melancholy, it just happened, a feeling of foreboding. Something was wrong and as the first bolt of lightning crackled through the grey, a single blood soaked wolf approached us.

'Give me a bow,' ordered Rognvaldr.

'No, leave him alone,' I had to shout to be heard, and I raised my hand to make sure they understood. I dropped from Thunder's back and slowly approached Gunnolf. He stood motionless; his yellow eyes staring as the rain diluted the blood that ran down his grey fur like crimson teardrops. I felt no threat, only a deep sadness.

'Helga, what are you doing?' I did not answer Rognvaldr, fearing Gunnolf might run away or attack me. Like Guthrom had said earlier, *'an injured wolf is dangerous,'* so I approached the wolf cautiously. I got within ten paces. Then Gunnolf turned to leave. He ran a scant distance and stopped, turning and staring at me. I moved forward again, and he repeated the action. He wanted me to follow him, so I did.

We ran side by side, and the others followed. I could feel his urgency and as he panted, I too gasped gulps of air, that pained by throat and burned my lungs. Yet, the pain was nothing compared to what I felt when I found Groa.

I hated the Gods when my mother died; I hated them when they took me from my home, and even these new gods too were determined that I should hate them as well. As the rain fell, so my heart sank, as I tried to comprehend the horror that lay in front of me.

Groa had been butchered and had died a hideous death. They had split her torso in two from between her legs up to her breasts. She was naked and her bloody entrails lay beside her cold, damp corpse. Gunnolf licked her face as if trying to revive her, but he could smell her death and was just reluctant to let her go. I stroked his head, and he whined.

This was beyond cruel, I thought. What had she said or done to deserve this, I wondered? She was a healer and seer and from what I had been told, her skills were well known throughout this land, yet here she lay brutally slaughtered. I knelt at her feet and started pulling her guts and internal organs towards me; then as gently as I could, I placed them back inside her. I just wanted her to be whole again. Her organs were still warm to the touch, so she had not been dead for long. Even in the gloom of twilight I could see the blood on my hands and, as the smell of her disembowelment engulfed me, my stomach heaved. Vomit burned my throat as the remnants of fish and bread added to the pungent aroma of death. More vomit followed until the contents of my stomach had been regurgitated. Even then, I still retched.

'Helga, come away, I will deal with this.'

I had not noticed the others arrive, but as Guthrom pulled at my shoulder, my grief gave way. There were no tears, just anger.

'No, I will do it,' I spat, 'leave me alone.' Guthrom removed his hand but did not withdraw.

'Then let me help.' His calmness and serene manner dowsed my ire slightly, and I nodded, accepting his offer.

'Why would they do this Guthrom?'

'I don't know, but Oddvar must pay for this.'

'Do you think he has killed Hella too?'

'No, he can sell Hella like he did my daughter. I'm sure she still lives. We must try to get her back.' I was shaking now. Memories flooded my mind, and I feared that I was going to fall apart. Guthrom held me tight 'You're ok, I have you.'

As darkness fell, we buried Groa. We carried her to a tiny hill that overlooked the river; it was Rognvaldr's idea, and it served the purpose well. If there were a life after death, then from this vantage point, she would see the sunrise and sunset and watch the moon play with the river's tides. Here she could converse with the gods and weave her magic for all of eternity.

I thought back to our conversation in her cave. Her words

echoed in my mind. She had spoken about my clouded destiny, my uncontrolled anger and the cost of my revenge and I had said I didn't care. But now, as I marked her grave with a circle of stones, I did care, I cared a lot, and said I was sorry. As I positioned the last pebble; the thunder came, and I knew then that Freja had welcomed Groa her into her hall. She had told me that Hella had her own path to follow, so I wondered if she had seen her own death within the flames. Hella lived, I was sure of it, but I feared the whispers that now gasped warnings at me from beyond the darkness. The Gods were talking.

CHAPTER TWENTY

It took longer than I thought to reach the farm, and although I kept looking, there had been no sign of Hella and so I figured Guthrom was probably right. Oddvar had seen value in the girl and had taken her with him. I only hoped that when he came for me, he would bring her with him.

Rognvaldr had been gone for a while, and I anxiously bit my nails as I sat with Guthrom and waited. A few of Rognvaldr's men were with us; they chatted amongst themselves, seemingly unperturbed by the events that were unravelling before us; within the walls of the derelict farm, we built a small fire. It spat in annoyance as droplets of rain found their way through the thatched roof and threw themselves into the flames below.

At the far side of the building, the walls lay in ruin, giving us an unobstructed view of the valley that stretched out into a black void of darkness. I strained my eyes as I scoured the landscape, searching for any sign of the horseman, but as yet, there was nothing.

'They will come, Helga,' Guthrom whispered, sensing my unease, whilst warming his hands over the spitting flames.

'What if they don't come? Things have hardly gone to plan since we left Vestfold, have they?'

It was true. What started out as a simple trip to Groa's cave, had now turned into total chaos and desperation. Death chased us and losing Groa now weighed heavily upon my conscience.

'Yes, that is true,' Guthrom agreed. 'Yet fate has brought us here, whatever the reason. Maybe it is our time to die; or maybe we will earn a magnificent victory and the skalds will sing songs of our incredible triumph. How Helga Red-hair led a small army through Gaulardal and defeated the mighty Heggalund and his hoard of warriors.'

I looked at him, expecting to see a mocking grin across his

bearded face, yet there was none.

'You believe that?' I asked, needing his reassurance.

'They will come, and together we will avenge Groa's death, but not before Oddvar tells me where my daughter is.'

I had forgotten all about Guthrom's daughter. The events of the previous days had overshadowed her plight until now. He was obsessed with finding her, and this had given his life a new purpose. He knew it was a long shot. She could be anywhere, but he didn't care, and I had made a promise to help him look for her and I would keep that promise, unless fate decreed otherwise.

'What makes you think Oddvar will remember her? It was a long time ago,' I asked.

'He might not remember my daughter, but he will know where she went to. I'm sure of it, and after he tells me all that I need to know, then we will kill him.'

I wanted to talk more, not just about Svanhild, but also about everything that had happened since leaving Vestfold. However, the appearance of horsemen exiting the valley cut me off.

'It's them.' Guthrom rose to his feet and made to leave, not wanting to, but aware that his presence would give us away.

'Stay calm and stay safe, I will find you.'

All I could do was nod as he left. This was my idea, and there was no turning back now. The others stayed with me, four in all. Each one a warrior whose instructions were to keep me safe at all times. I was supposed to be their prisoner, so they loosely bound my hands behind my back, but a sharp tug would release them when the fighting started. I was not expected to fight; I was just the bait, but they had hidden a shield and sword under fallen thatch, along with my dagger, should the need arise.

Oddvar was a very cautious man; even though Rognvaldr had only fifty warriors with him, his mistrust was obvious.

Everyone dismounted from their horses and two lines of

well-armed men gathered round as I was taken from the dilapidated building and paraded in front of his men.

'So this is Helga, daughter to a King, she looks more like a Hundorp whore to me,' he smirked, so I smiled.

'This whore slit Kvist's throat and watched him die, it was not an honourable death.' He leered at me but ignored my boast.

'Where are the others?' he asked.

'Others?' Rognvaldr repeated.

'Don't take me as a fool. Where are her companions?'

'It was difficult enough to smuggle her out, let alone the others. She is the one that will bring ransom, the others are mere trinkets. Either you want her or you don't. I can take her back. There is still time.' Rognvaldr grabbed my arm, and with his men, started back towards the building. He had realized that we were out in the open and too far from the tree line for Guthrom and the others to spring a surprise attack.

'Wait,' Oddvar yelped. He menacingly walked towards us and his men followed close behind. Grasping the handle of his sword, he removed it from its sheath. His men followed suit. We turned to face them but continued to retreat towards the trees. Our warriors quickly formed a shield wall in front of us as Rognvaldr removed his dagger and placed it at my throat.

'I will kill her,' he shouted. Then whispered in my ear,

'When I say, run to the building.' I tugged at my bindings and released my hands, but kept them behind my back.

'You're an idiot boy. You honestly think I give a shit about making coin from a bitch like her. I came back with you to take her, dead or alive it matters not to me. She killed my friend and took my slave, so I figure I should have the pleasure of humping it a few times, before I gut her like I did the witch.'

I wanted to kill him there and then and be done with it, but this was not the time for rash decisions, so I held firm, comforted that Rognvaldr was beside me.

'Look, I'm a reasonable man; you're all going to die, anyway. Whether it's today, tomorrow, or the next day. So give me the girl now, and you can all go back to Hundorp. Heggalund is coming, and when he arrives, there will be no mercy for any of you. He will slaughter every man, woman and child in your settlement. However, as a token of our deal, I will ask him to spare your miserable lives, you and your men, now give me the girl.'

'Run,'

The ground was slippery from the constant rain. I almost fell, but a powerful hand pulled me up and dragged me towards the farm building. Once inside, I removed the thatch and grabbed the shield and sword that was hidden earlier, whilst placing my dagger in its familiar place against my leg. Running through the rear of the building, we formed a small shield wall as Oddvar and his men rounded the building and faced us down. I urgently looked round for Guthrom and the others, but could see no movement amongst the trees.

'Where are they?' I looked at Rognvaldr, but he said nothing.
We just continued to retreat, slowly and with shields raised.

When the eagle hunts, it appears suddenly on silent wings,
gliding quietly until it hammers into its prey, surprising it, then
slicing it apart with bladed talons. When Guthrom and the
others came, it was like the eagle. They came not from the trees.
They had used the cover of darkness to outflank Oddvar's men
and approached from beyond the farm instead. As they
attacked Rognvaldr urged us forward, Oddvar had nowhere to
go. Guthrom reached them first, slamming into them. Shield to
shield, they pushed them hard toward our own shield wall. Our
enemy was disorganized and dismayed and although some
turned to face our advance, they were few, and we were many,
and they died quickly as our swords and axes sliced them apart.
This was my first taste of battle and as we surrounded our

quarry, I got my first kill.

A gap had appeared in our wall as two men slipped on the rain-soaked grass. I watched as several of Oddvar's men pushed through it before it was closed behind them. As the men on the ground attempted to rise, an axe-carrying warrior stepped forward and dispatched them. He was tall and fearless, and although he knew he would surely die, he seemed oblivious to this fact. He growled like a bear as he raised his axe high above his head before gleefully crashing it down, slicing the man's face in two before moving to the next. I could hear the cracking of bone above the noise of battle, and for an instant I froze. The darkness hid the blood, but I felt it spray onto my face as the giant turned to strike at the other man, who raised his shield in a futile attempt to deflect the blow. His shield shattered, his arm with it and now defenceless, the killing blow almost sliced him from shoulder to waist.

Instinctively and with all sense of self-preservation gone, the ice melted away. I ran hard and fast and with all my strength slammed my shield into his side on. Sensing my arrival, he turned at the last minute, just enough to absorb the impact. He kept his balance as I lashed out desperately with my sword. He easily deflected the blow, so I attempted another, but again, he defended well. I took two steps back and breathed deeply.

He looked at me and laughed as he stepped towards me. I backed off, thinking I should probably run; I was no match for this beast. Sensing my fear, he charged, axe in hand, a bringer of death. Too late to run now, I thought. Speed and agility were my only weapon and, as the axe fell, I moved and parried, ducking low. It was the slightest of blows, but it was enough. As he slipped past me, I sliced my sword across the back of his legs and he crumbled like a felled tree. I didn't hesitate, I leapt forward, and with both hands, plunged my sword into his leather clad back. There was no scream, only an expulsion of air, and as his head turned to the side, his eyes stared at me. I had used so much force that my sword skewered him hilt deep. Its blade had not only penetrated his body, but it had also stuck into the ground beneath. Putting my foot on his blood soaked back, it took me several attempts before it finally broke free. The giant gasped and reached for his axe that had fallen from his grip. He could not move, and I could see the panic in his eyes as he realized his weapon was out of reach. A seat in Odin's hall awaited him, but I denied it and kicked the axe further from his grip. He was Oddvar's man and together they had cruelly butchered Groa, who was not only my friend, but was Erik's mother too. There would be no feasting with the gods for this man.

Reaching down, I removed my dagger, and whilst straddling my prey, I pulled at his lice matted hair, baring his throat. My blade is always sharp and as I pulled it across his naked throat. A wolf howled and knew it was Gunnolf. He was watching me, hidden deep within the darkness, and he cried once more before

I dispatched his revenge.

Looking around, I noticed the fighting had ceased, and that we had prevailed.

'You fight well for a woman,' a man shouted as he approached me.

'My name is Finnulf and you have to be Helga, daughter of Harald Fairhair. You are building yourself quite a reputation. I was there when you kicked Sigurd's arse. That was amazing, but this,' he pointed at the fallen warrior, 'is truly beyond words.'

When he smiled, his face wrinkled, which made him look older than he probably was. Unlike most of the men, he was beardless and although his hair was long; he had tied it in a long ponytail, giving him a more feminine appearance. He was thin, with narrow features like a weasel, but I sensed intelligence and ambition behind his dark brown eyes.

'I am Helga yes, so you were just watching, not fighting

Finnulf? I could have done with your help.'

'Oh, I can fight but only when needs must, you seemed to be handling yourself pretty well, so I left you to it. I have other skills, some of which you may find useful in the future.' He smiled and aged ten summers.

'Really? And what skills would they be?' I asked.

'You will see when the time is right.'

CHAPTER TWENTY-ONE

I walked through the dead and dying, Finnulf by my side. I had never seen the remnants of battle before, and although this was a mere skirmish; the scene was filled with decapitation and gore. The smell of blood, shit and piss filled my nostrils and my stomach lurched, spewing all its contents from my gaping mouth.

Finnulf laughed whilst patting my back hard, causing even more regurgitation. Only moments ago, I was slitting a man's throat, his blood oozing through my fingers without thought or care, but now, as the genuine horror descended and my adrenalin waned, it hit me hard. Combat had exhilarated me; I had felt the blood lust in my veins and heard my sword sing with delight. But now, as I looked at the bodies that lay scattered about me, I understood why men believed the shield wall was not a place for a woman. Yet, for me to exert my revenge and take my place amongst men, it would have to become my home and I would have to get used to seeing these fields of slaughter.

As my stomach settled and the sickliness faded, Guthrom and Rognvaldr approached.

'Are you all right?' asked Rognvaldr. He cradled my face, his eyes betraying concern and something more.

'I'm fine,' I gasped, breathing deeply to blow the nausea away.

'She fought bravely, and slaughtered a mighty beast,' Finnulf explained excitedly, patting my back once more.

'Do that again and I will kill you, you piece of weasel shit.' His annoying laugh filled the night's air as he walked away, disappearing into the night like a ghostly apparition.

Rognvaldr then tried to embrace me, but I pushed him away.

'Not here, not in front of the men.' I didn't want to seem any weaker than I had already shown by emptying my stomach. I felt embarrassed, but those feeling soon dissipated when I saw that Oddvar still lived.

Rage can overwhelm you; it can make you act impulsively, without thought, consideration and without care. A seed had been planted on my island five years earlier. It had grown within me and now it was bursting out. Its influence flowered into every segment of my being. I was rage filled and as my heart raced and head pounded; I lashed out.

My sword was moments from a killing blow when Erik, shield in his hand, blocked it. He laughed.

'Guthrom said you would do that.' Manara stepped in front of me.

'Get out of my way,' I spat, but Manara stood firm.

'Helga,' she breathed. 'You promised Guthrom, calm down.'

I turned to face Guthrom,

'Do you really think this turd will lead you to your daughter? He won't, she is gone, sold as a slave or a whore. She could be anywhere and Oddvar hasn't a fucking clue where she is, nor does he care. He sliced Groa to pieces, just for the hell of it, and I intend to do the same to him.'

'That may be true Helga, but there is more at stake here. He has information about Heggalund's army and where he plans to attack. He will say nothing unless his life is spared and he can speak directly to Eystein in Hundorp.'

I shook my head. This was Kvist all over again. Turning away, I saw an injured enemy trying to crawl away through the bodies of battle. I was so upset that all rationality had evaporated from me as walked purposely over to him. He must have sensed my approach and turn onto his back to face me.

'Please,' he begged, raising his hands, but I was in no mood for compassion. I plunged my sword into his gut, knowing it would not kill him instantly. Then slowly and cruelly, I turned the blade in my hands, enjoying his screaming and smiling insanely as his eyes bulged and lips quivered. I then pulled the blade south towards his groin. I glared at Oddvar and saw him staring back at me. I was revelling in the madness as the warrior whimpered like a scolded dog. It was then that Rognvaldr stepped in, and as the axe fell, his screams ceased. I stopped what I was doing and looked at my lover. His blank expression spoke volumes.

  'We leave for Hundorp, get your horse.' His tone was authoritative; gone was the concern and love that he had shown me moments earlier. He moved away, and the others followed, leaving me alone with the dead. I sank to my knees with both hands still gripping my sword tightly. Placing my head against them, I allowed my anger to subside. A raging storm had swirled inside my heart, a hurricane of hatred; it was my nature, uncontrolled and relentless. It scared me, for I was not always aware of my brutality. I could be so cruel, lost in my madness. Then, as the seas calmed, and the clouds parted, I would return to my former self, the little girl that had once strolled along the beach and played amongst the standing stones.

The journey back to Hundorp was a quiet one; I paused briefly near the hill where Groa now lay; Erik and Manara kept me company, and together we watched the sun rise and I wondered what had happened to Hella. I felt drained and was thankful that Thunder bore my weight; I ran my hands through his hair and noticed the dried blood of my enemies between my fingers.

'Are you all right, Helga? You seem distracted?' Erik knew me so well. There was a bond between us, like a brother and sister, and he knew I was troubled.

'Do you remember when we were on the boat and you lifted me on your shoulders?'

'I do, what of it.'

'I cursed Heggalund that day and swore I would have my vengeance; I asked Thor for his help. Do you remember?'

Erik nodded.'I do.'

'Well, I now worry about the cost, Erik. How many more of us must die just so as I can be satisfied? And what if the Gods decide Heggalund is more worthy of their support than I am.' Erik paused before he answered.

'If my mother had died at the hands of another, I too would feel as you do. I wouldn't rest till I had reaped my revenge or died trying. Sometimes fate has a way of leading us down a twisted path that crosses many bridges. Some lead us away, while others bring us closer, but at some point, we reach our destination. You will lose some and gain others on your journey, it's just the way of it.' He was looking towards the hill, and the rising sun bathed his face in an orange glow. I wanted so much to tell him that Groa was his mother, but I had made her a promise, and I intended to keep her secret.

'You should be a seer with wisdom like that,' I jested.

'Nah, I prefer being the handsome warrior that women can't

resist.' I laughed, and Manara blushed.

CHAPTER TWENTY-TWO

Hundorp was a hive of activity when we arrived; it looked like Eystein had been successful at gathering warriors, and we would need every one of them when the time came.

'Where have you been, brother? Father wants to see you.' Sigurd had been waiting for our return and stood with a small band of men who had just arrived by boat. He looked at me but said nothing. I smiled, and he lowered his head sheepishly.

We pushed our way through the throng and made to the great hall where Eystein was deep in conversation. Aseda noticed our arrival and tugged at her husband's arm. The King rose to his feet and did not look well pleased.

'Where the hell have you been?' He growled.

'Father, if I could explain.' Rognvaldr stuttered.

'Please do, but I bet it has something to do with her,' he pointed an accusing finger in my direction and like a naughty child I looked down to the floor, guilty as accused.

Guthrom saved us, pushing Oddvar through the crowded room and presenting him to the King.

'My lord; Oddvar has some interesting information he would like to share with you.' The King looked at Oddvar, who smiled and bowed his head slightly as the King approached.

Eystein said nothing. He just stood in front of Oddvar with his hands tucked neatly behind his back and waited for the trader to speak, which he did after Guthrom prodded him forcefully.

'My Lord, it is good to see you again,' Oddvar lied.

Oh, I so wanted to kill him, and cursed Guthrom for denying me that satisfaction, but I listened intently as he spoke, hoping that he had some revelation that was worth his life.

'Jarl Heggalund is coming; he is going to take your Kingdom my lord. You are all going to die, and all your woman and children will be enslaved.'

Silence followed as Oddvar stood rigidly. His smile faded and was replaced by a stern defiant gaze that was fixated on the King. 'He has over two thousand men gathered from three petty kingdoms and awaits five hundred more from a fourth. You have what, four hundred shields at most? I suggest you release me, Eystein Glumra, so I can inform him that you wish to support his cause, rather than fight against it. You may lose your Kingdom, but you may just keep your life and that of your people, minus a few of your more valuable assets.' He looked towards Åseda and bowed his head arrogantly. He was so confident of his own self-importance and he had a good right to be, we were in what seemed like a hopeless position.

He expected the blow; in fact, he seemed to demand it, but it wasn't Glumra that reacted. It was Rognvaldr, and the punch to the side of his head was so forceful that it sent him sprawling across the floor. Dazed, he attempted to get up, but the foot that connected shattered his jaw and if it hadn't been for the King, he would have surely died there and then at Rognvaldr's hand.

'Enough Rognvaldr. Take him away and guard him well, we may still have a use for him.' The King gestured to two of his men, who grabbed the barely conscious Oddvar and removed him from the hall.

'My Lord,' Guthrom interjected. 'Oddvar told me that Heggalund plans to spit his forces, sending half south to face Harald and the rest through the valley to Hundorp.'

'So, what's your point? It's still at least a thousand men, and I have but five hundred at my. disposal, and of them, only three hundred have regularly seen a shieldwall. We cannot defeat Jarl Heggalund Guthrom. Oddvar is right.'

'Forgive me, lord, I mean no offence, but I have to disagree. I admit, with such a huge number of men at his disposal, our fate may seem sealed. However, we now know that Heggalund is waiting for more warriors to arrive. This could work in our favour. It may give us the time required for Grjotgardsson to arrive from Hladir. That will give us around eight hundred shields, maybe a few more.' Eystein raised his hand.

'Guthrom, your figures are hopeful at best, and we would still face a thousand shields or more. The situation is hopeless. So I will talk to Heggalund.' There was a huge reaction within the hall. Voices were raised as some agreed with their king, yet many more did not, shouting that they would prefer to die than be ruled by Heggalund.

'King Glumra,' Guthrom shouted, raising his voice to be heard over the throng that still rankled with each other. His tone demanding silence in the room. I wondered if Guthrom had gone too far for it. Was no way to address a King. Eystein however, did not react. Instead he wearily lowered himself into his seat, waving a resigning hand allowing Guthrom to continue.

Guthrom bowed his head, lowered his voice, and continued.

'Forgive my outburst Lord King; but If we are to have any

chance of a victory, we need to be united, and we need to face

them all. Every single one of them, two thousand warriors or

more, it makes no difference. What matters the most, is that we

make them fight us where we want them to. Not here but where

the valley is at its narrowest. That is where we must make our

stand, fight, and pray to all our Gods, that King Harald brings

us a thousand men or more from the south before we all fall. If

he does that, then there is hope; if not, then we will all journey

to Valhalla together.'

 We all looked at Eystein, waiting for his response. He in turn

looked at Åseda, who just smiled and reached for his hand.

'You're either all mad or drunk,' gasped Eystein. 'Even if I

agree to your ludicrous plan; why would they all come through

the valley? When half of their numbers would be enough to

defeat us? It is a ridiculous idea.' Glumra turned away,

exasperated by the suggestion.

'They would come for her my Lord,' the King glanced back to

see Guthrom pointing at me, and laughed mockingly.

'Why would Heggalund do that? She is nothing to him. Once he defeats Harald, she is worthless, and will probably become the slave she was always meant to be.'

He was wrong, and both Guthrom and I knew it.

'He will come,' I said confidently. 'I can make him come, and when he brings all his men through the valley, we can trap him; like a wolf pack traps a deer. Then when my father arrives from the south, there will be a great slaughter. The valley will flood with the blood of our enemies and I will kill Heggalund.' I spoke calmly and believed every word. 'Guthrom is right. We must face them all. If we are all going to die, then let it be glorious. I am a slave to no man, my Lord, and I would rather fight with you and your people than suffer such an indignity. I was born a Pict; my people fought the great Roman Empire and prevailed. They defeated enormous armies, some even bigger than Heggalund's. They were cunning, brave, fearless and brutal, but the one thing that stirred their souls the most, was that they were fighting for their home, their women and their children. I am no longer a Pict; I am Norse, but our position is the same as the Picts. We must fight for our home, for the Kingdom; and for our King.'

The hall erupted, Glumra's men cheered and thumped the tables and benches. Inside, my heart was pounding and shaking in my chest, but my exterior was calm and I fixed my eyes on the King.

'Helga, you are Wolf mad, like an Ulfheonar,' he said, which I liked. It seemed fitting as Groa's wolf, Gunnolf, had taken a liking to me and I always felt he was nearby, watching over me, albeit from a distance.

'So be it, we will make our stand in Gaulardal.'

The room rang out again with cheers at the King's decision.

'Fetch ale, for if I'm to die tomorrow, I want to be drunk today.' He sat down next to Åseda and as they filled his drinking horn, he raised it above his head. 'For Odin.' He bellowed and the name of their one-eyed god reverberated around the room as men drank and woman poured.

Erik handed me a drink.

'For Thor,'

'For Thor,' I repeated before downing the bitter ale in one go.

'Ha, you may drink like a man, Helga, but you don't fight like one,' he teased.

'No Erik, I fight like a woman, which makes me even more deadly.' We laughed and spent the rest of the day drinking until my head swam and my legs buckled. I remember little more of that day, but when I woke up, it was dark and Rognvaldr lay naked next to me.

It was icy cold, as I slipped from beneath the bearskin. I had an overwhelming urge to piss, but did not understand where I was and what to piss in, and so I went outside. The darkness engulfed me as I nakedly tiptoed towards the river, looking for some foliage to hide behind so that I could relieve myself.

'Your skin is paler than that of the moon. I thought you were a ghost.'

I jumped, then stumbled, drunkenly landing on my bare arse, my legs splayed.

'Thanks for the offer,' Sigurd said, 'but you're too skinny for my liking, I like a woman with tits.' I struggled to my feet and failed miserably to cover the vital areas.

'Here you can borrow this,' he said throwing me his jacket. He was being kind, and I wondered if I had damaged his head more than I had realized. I pulled on his jacket and was relieved that its size covered the parts that mattered the most.

'Tell me Helga, why are you here? I admit your words were inspiring, I almost cheered myself. It seems you have a way of getting what you want, even my father bends his will for you. Yet I believe you care nothing for my people or my family. You will get us all killed Helga, and for what.'

My befuddled head was clearing, thanks to the chilly breeze that whipped across the river and slapped my youthful cheeks.

'Sigurd, I am here not through choice, but because the Gods willed it, and it is not me that will kill your people, it is Heggalund that will do that.' I paused, rushing to a nearby tree as I could hold on no longer.

'Don't piss on my jacket, I don't want your smell hanging around me.' I ignored him and squatted.

'Tell me, Sigurd,' I yelled. 'Have you met Heggalund?' My question unnerved him.

'You accuse me of treachery? Be careful.' He spat.

'I did not. I asked if you had met him, that's all. I accused you of nothing, but you react with guilt.' I was pushing him without realizing the danger I was putting myself in, being naked with just a jacket for protection.

'I have met some of his men. They said their Jarl makes them rich and treats them well. He provides plenty of ale and women.

What more does a man require?' he smirked like the Sigurd of old.

I left my watering place and moved towards him.

'Your father gives you the same, does he not?' I asked.

'Ha ale yes, but not women, I find them myself,' he boasted.

'I like your father, your mother, too. I was not aware that Åseda was Asa's sister. That almost makes us related, Sigurd.' He responded by expelling air through his lips, attempting to discount any family connection. 'Your Father loves his people and his sons; you should treasure that; for Heggalund cares for nobody but himself. He is a monster and you should be wary of him.' My contempt overflowed, and I spat the last few words.

'Maybe so; or maybe it is your hatred towards him we should be wary of, more than the man himself. I heard he killed you mother and destroyed your village when you were a child. Revenge can be a powerful tool, but it can also drown you in your own madness. Maybe the same monster lurks inside of you too.'

It shocked me that Sigurd compared me to Heggalund. So I removed his jacket and threw it at him before storming off naked, back to Rognvaldr. As each angry footstep slapped on the cold ground, I wondered if some of what Sigurd said was true. Maybe a monster did resided within me.

CHAPTER TWENTY-THREE

It may have been the warm sun on my back that gently woke me from a dream filled sleep, that or Rognvaldr's fingers caressing my right breast, teasing the nipple till erect, much like his swollen manhood that nudged at my buttocks teasing them apart.

'Not now,' I whispered. 'My head pounds like a blacksmith's hammer. I need some water.' I dragged my body from the warm bed and found a flask. It was warm, but I didn't care. It cured my dry mouth and cleared my somewhat befuddled brain. I wiped the drops from my lips, which Rognvaldr found amusing, the look in his eye and a wicked smirk, made me realize that it reminded him of the night before, of which I had no recollection at all.

It took me a while to dress. Firstly because of the overindulgence of ale and, second, because Rognvaldr kept trying to persuade me back into bed. Thankfully, the intense rapping at the door demanded attention, and Rognvaldr reluctantly answered it.

'Cinead, what is it?' The concern in his voice caused me to join him. Upon seeing Cinead's face, I knew something was wrong.

'What is it?' I asked.

'It's Hella. The scouts found her in Gaulardal.'

'She's dead?' I feared the worse after finding Groa, but Cinead shook his head.

'No, she's alive, barely.'

'Where is she?' I felt panicked and could tell by Cinead's demeanour that something was very wrong. 'Where is she?' I screamed.

'She's with the Queen.'

I quickly dressed and ran through the huts, pushing people aside in my haste. The great hall appeared in front of me. There was a crowd and as I reached the entrance, Guthrom grabbed me.

'Let me past I want to see her,' I pleaded, but Guthrom held firm. He spoke quietly but firmly and would not loosen his grip.

'Not yet. You must wait. Aseda is tending to her wounds. She is weak, but alive. We may have to thank your wolf for that.'

'Gunnolf? Where is he?'

'Gone, but he has a knack for appearing when he's needed most. Hella would surely have died without him. He kept her warm and protected her from scavengers until the scouts found them both. Luckily, one of them had been with us when we found Groa and recognized him, persuading him to leave the child rather than face an arrow.'

'Guthrom, I need to see her now, please.' He relented and escorted me through the hall and into the King's quarters. Aseda looked up as we entered. Tears streamed down her face. Hella lay naked on the bed. There was not one part of her body that was not bruised, broken, or beaten. I drifted closer, fearing that even my movements could inflict more pain and suffering on the child. From head to toe, she was damaged, externally and internally, gang raped and abused by more than one. Marks on her ankles and wrists showed she had been tethered and stretched, and I winced at her contorted joints. Thankfully, she was unconscious as I knelt by the bed and stroked her tangled hair.

'Oh Hella, I'm sorry I wasn't there to protect you.' I whispered.

My eyes scanned her once more, and as I noticed the finger marks around her neck, I felt my monster rise.

Hella would live, although as the years passed, she may wish she had died. I left the hall without saying another word, and Guthrom followed.

As I exited the hall, Rognvaldr approached. He had heard about Hella, and his face showed genuine concern.

'She is in excellent hands, I'm sure she will be fine,' his attempt at consoling me was futile.

'She will never be fine,' I spat. I was angry. In fact, I was beyond angry. Every God, every man filled me with hate. At that moment, I cursed them all and screamed my hatred to the heavens for Odin to hear. Rognvaldr tried to comfort me, but I lashed out, not wanting his touch anywhere near me.

'Helga, calm yourself,' urged Guthrom.

'I will not,' I screamed. 'Where is Oddvar? Take me to him.'

'I understand your anger, but you are not thinking straight.' His response did not have a calming effect.

'Oh yes, I forgot we must protect him, keep him safe, even though you yourself said he must die after what he did to Groa, yet still he lives and why Guthrom? I shall tell you, he lives because you believe he knows where Svanhild is. Well, let me tell you, he knows your weakness, he can smell your desperation and he will say anything to save his putrid life, just like Kvist. You've seen Hella, do you think Svanhild got off lightly, that she was something special, maybe she was worth more, deserving to be fucked by one man rather than a whole fucking army.' I stepped forward and faced Guthrom down.

'Take me to Oddar or I will tear down every hut and barn in Hundrop until I find him. I want this Guthrom and I won't let you or anyone else stand in my way.'

He did not move, he just stared at me, his eyes blank and distant. There was no warmth, only cold consideration.

'He is in the barn with the horses. Erik and Manara are with him.'

I pushed my way past him and ran down towards the barn as Guthrom shouted after me.

'Your hate will destroy you Helga, first Heggalund, now Oddvar, who's next on your list?' I ignored him because he was a man and men ignore the suffering of a woman. Only a woman could understand what Hella had been through. Åseda knew, for her tears were pain filled and reflected her anguish. I knew it too, but my tears had long since become resistant to feelings of heartache. Guthrom was right. I was filled me with hate, and Oddvar was about to feel every part of it.

When I arrived at the stables, Erik was alone. He was feeding the horses after giving them a wash down. Thunder, annoyed at being wet, shook himself vigorously, splashing me in the process. Another time I would have found that amusing, but not today.

Oddvar was sitting in a corner, his legs tied but his hands free as he ate a bowl of cold leftover stew and bread.

'Tie his hands then leave us Erik,' I ordered, 'make sure nobody enters.' Erik stopped what he was doing.

'Guthrom told me…'

I cut him off abruptly. 'I don't give a shit what Guthrom said.' I turned and faced my friend, whose expression showed confusion and uncertainty.

'Erik,' I softened my tone through gritted teeth. 'I need to speak with Oddvar, on my own and with no interruptions. You can wait for me outside until I am done. Let no one inside.' Erik hesitated, then conceded and left.

Finally, I was alone with Oddvar and as he smiled at me through stew-covered lips; I stepped purposefully towards him.

'Helga Haraldsdottir, the flame haired bitch that killed Kvist, have you come to say sorry?'

'I've come to kill you, you piece of filth.' I was in no hurry and intended to make him suffer until he begged to die.

'Oh, I see. What does Guthrom think of that? He won't be happy with you if you kill me, for I know of his daughter's whereabouts. So, If I die, he will never know, and will hate you for the rest of his life.' He laughed and I could not resist kicking him in the face, my boot cracking his nose and removing a few of his smirking teeth.

'Oh, how brave you are,' he mocked, 'kicking a man when he's down. Untie me bitch and I will rip you apart with my bare hands.'

'Tell me, rassragr did Groa tell you that I was going to kill you? I think she did. That is why you gutted her. You feared her, didn't you? And so told Guthrom a lie, thinking It would change your fate.'

'I fear no one, especially you, wench. You're not even from these shores. You are like a bitch with worms, a shit-stained smear on our grasslands. Why don't you pay for a boat and take your fish smelling arse back where you came from?' He spat at me, but it fell well short.

'I think your scared, Oddvar. You killed Groa and sacrificed her to Odin, hoping to appease the All father, but you have made a grave mistake. Groa was a servant of Freya, not Odin, and the Goddess is so angry with you that she has sent me to punish you for your murdering ways. Not only that, but you abused one of Freya's children and for that, you must suffer in ways you can't imagine. Kvist was lucky I killed him quickly; you, on the other hand…' I let my words trail off while he considered his fate.

'I did not touch the child,' he finally said.

'So who did? Heggalund?' I wanted him to say yes, to give my monster even more reason to hate that name.

'No, I gave her to my men. Those that still wait for me in Gaulardal. If I don't return soon, they will think me dead and leave to join the Jarl. Most will march south to meet Harald in battle, and once more, you will become homeless and orphaned. It is your destiny.'

I watched as he hauled himself into a sitting. position, placing his back against a wooden beam, blood dribbling from his nose, mouth, and lips. I smiled at him as I dropped onto my haunches.

'Before I killed Kvist, I spoke with Groa in her cave. She told me my destiny, and she said nothing about being orphaned. In fact, she told me I would have my revenge on Heggalund and one-day travel home to the place of my birth. I think she told you something too, and you didn't like it. You thought by killing her, you could alter your fate. Yet here you sit in a shit-covered barn, waiting to die by my hand. Ha… how fickle the gods can be.' I stood back up and unsheathed my knife.

'You need me girl, Guthrom needs me.' He was fidgeting and realizing that his bargaining power had diminished.

'No, I don't need you at all, and Guthrom only thinks he does. Groa told me where you took Svanhild and after Heggalund is dead, I will travel there and bring her home. It has been foretold.' I said mockingly.

'You will die in Dyflin, it is not like here. You and the cripple will be slaughtered without my help.' He laughed, but it was a nervous laugh, which faded as I moved my knife towards his left eye.

'Dyflin? thank you Oddvar.'

He realized then, that any hold on his life had just disappeared completely. I had fooled him into telling me where Svanhild was, and as my blade entered his eye socket; he knew he was going to die.

His screams reminded me of the foxes that lived on my island, loud and haunting, as if in distress. Oddvar was very distressed, enough for Erik to rush in to see what the hell was going on. He stopped in his tracks when he saw the bloody mess that lay before him. Oddvar was still alive. I made sure of that. I had removed his eye, an ear and both his balls and was just slicing through his cock when Erik entered.

'Helga, what are you doing?' Erik gasped. 'For the love of Thor, kill him.'

'No… not yet. I want him to suffer like Groa and Hella did. If you can't stomach it, then get out.'

I was covered in Oddvar's blood and must have looked

demented, but I cared not. Erik left, and I knew he would fetch Guthrom or Cinead, but it didn't matter because Oddvar would be dead by the time they arrived. I had one more thing to do.

Oddvar lay on his side, whimpering like a castrated dog. I knelt by his head and stroked his blood-soaked hair.

'Shush, quiet yourself. It will soon be over,' I whispered. He mumbled something, but it was inaudible, his life was draining away so I acted swiftly, one the last thrust.

His leather trousers could not resist the point of my blade as it split his pants and entered his anus. Oddvar had one more scream left in him as I pushed gently, slowly penetrating him fraction by fraction until my knife's blade disappeared. A combination of blood and shit oozed from the wound. He gasped, gurgled and as the hilt of my knife reached his arse cheeks, he died.

'Hel is waiting for you, Oddvar.' I sneered as I ruthlessly withdrew my blade. I needed one more thing.

A knife is not the best tool for removing a head. I did not have the strength to remove it in one go, so I sliced and hacked at it, pulling and tugging until it eventually snapped from the rest of his body. The effort exhausted me. I sat next to what was left of his torso and cradled his head in my lap. I looked at it and thought what an ugly bastard Oddvar was; it was an absurd thought which made me giggle like a small child until the reality of my actions kicked in. My monster had left me, my anger withered, and now I was all that was left. I had killed Oddvar; I had done it cruelly and sadistically, and I had loved every moment.

CHAPTER TWENTY-FOUR

We knew they were coming, as Leif had arrived at first light with a smile wider than the river. People cheered and warriors clashed swords against shields to welcome Grjotgardsson and his men to Hundorp. The Jarl had brought many men, over four hundred, some mounted but most on foot. They had rallied to the call, and my heart danced with excitement as Hakon dismounted and hugged Åseda.

'I knew you would come, father,' she said, weeping tears of happiness tinged with a hint of relief.

'I would travel ten times as far for you and your sister,' he smiled and pulled her close once more.

'Hakon, it's good to see you,' Eystein extended a hand, which was well received.

'The messenger has told me of your need and that Harfagre is on route. What news do you have of his progress?'

'We have heard nothing. My scouts have seen no sign of his approach, although they are finding it hard to venture far because of Heggalund's men. They fill the valley.'

'I understand. How many swords do we have?' Eystein hesitated before answering.

'With your men, we have around nine hundred. The forces that gather against us number over two thousand, and as for Harfagre, his numbers are unknown. Guthrom reckons Vestfold can muster five hundred at least, but we prey to Odin that others will join him on the way.'

'Where are Guthrom and Helga?'

He looked for us, and we stepped forward to greet him.

'My lord, it is good to see you again it has been far too long,' Guthrom smiled as they embraced, which surprised Eystein.

'For the love of Freya, where has the child gone?' He laughed, hugging me tightly. I had met Hakon not long after I had arrived in Vestfold. He was kind to me and insisted I called him Grandfather.

'Asa has been feeding you too well, Helga, you are more woman than child now. Tell me Guthrom, has her wildness faded or matured with age?'

'Oh, she is as wild as ever my Lord, just more skilled and deadly with it.' I took that as a compliment, although I don't know if Guthrom meant it that way.

The others joined us and the Jarl greeted us all individually. His warmth was genuine, and I understood immediately where Asa and Aseda inherited their love and compassion from.

We retired inside the great hall, while the villages tended to the needs of the extra guests, bringing food and drink for the newly arrived army. Hundorp was overflowing, they found places for some, but many just sat at any available spot, enjoying the attention and welcoming the rest after a long march.

It was muggy outside, but within the hall, it was stifling. The smell of cooking, fish and sweat filled the space with pungent aromas; Hakon looked exhausted after his journey. He was not a young man, but Erik reckoned he was still a formidable warrior, regardless of his advancing years.

We all sat at the main table, and as the others chatted, I listened intently whilst nibbling some bread and cheese, washed down with warm ale.

'It's a shame we gather here under such circumstances Eystein, family visits should be a joyful affair.' Eystein nodded in agreement.

'Indeed, yet here we are and I have to ask you Hakon, how do you see my position. Guthrom assures me that my kingdom is safe if I give fealty to Harfagre. What do you say? You know the man better than I do.' Glumra was still concerned about my father and now shared his worries with his father-in-law.

'Tell me, Eystein, do you doubt my daughter's judgment?' his abruptness caught the King off guard.

'No, what is your point.' The accusation perturbed Glumra, and he shuffled uncomfortably in his seat.

'Åseda told me she wanted to be your wife because you were honourable, a kind man and a moral leader, so I allowed it to happen.' His Steely blue eyes stared directly at Eystein and his face was stern to say the least. 'What makes you think Asa does not possess the same judgment in a man as her sister does? Is Harald Harfagre less honourable than you? I agree he is ambitious, and yearns to unite our petty kingdoms under one King, and yes, he wants to be that King. But he cannot rule on his own, and he knows that. He needs men like us to support him, to help him reach such a lofty status. He has had much success both in war and diplomacy, and maybe we could all prosper under his leadership. Peace between our kingdoms would be a welcome change from the constant threat of wars. I for one am tired of the shield wall, and I would rather serve Harald willingly than meet him in battle. My advice to you is to listen to Guthrom; Harald is not someone you want for an enemy, Eystein.'

'This may be so, but without our help he would surely be defeated.' Eystein was trying in vain to defend his point of view, but he failed miserably.

'Without Harald's help, and mine, you, too, would be defeated. Are you willing to take that risk? I can always take my daughter back to Hladir with me.' Eystein was visibly bristled, but grudgingly accepted that Hakon was probably right. He had very few options at his disposal.

'Guthrom thinks we should lure them west through the valley and hold them there until Harald arrives from the South. A risky strategy, don't you think?' He was looking for support, but he was not going to receive it from Hakon.

'What other option do we have? I think Guthrom is right, but how do we convince them to do that? Heggalund is no fool.'

'I can make him come,' I whispered.

Hakon laughed and said I was moon mad, and maybe I was because I too wasn't sure if Heggalund would take the bait or not. I had a plan but nobody really wanted to hear it and I understood why; I was a woman and young, too. What did I know. Guthrom tried to intercede on my behalf, but his words fell on deaf ears, so as the ale flowed, they explored alternative ideas.

Whilst the men chatted amongst themselves, I moved away. A feeling of disappointment descended, as I realised that it would always be like this. I didn't really have a voice; nobody took me seriously. At the moment I felt so alone, and just for a moment I thought about leaving, then Erik joined me and I realised I couldn't.

'What is this plan you have, Helga?' Erik asked.

So, I told him.

'That is a good plan the best I have heard tonight.'

I smiled and wondered if he was just placating me.

'I'm serious Helga I do think he would come. If he didn't, he will look weak in front of his men and allies. How can he be the glorious leader of men if he fears a mere girl?' He laughed before adding, 'He should fear you though, I'm terrified of you, and I'm your friend.' He winked and I grabbed him tight.

'I thought I had lost you, Erik.' I mumbled, my emotions almost getting the better of me. He said nothing but held me tight, stroking my hair whilst kissing my forehead. Words were not required, our embrace said it all.

The night wore thin, and as the ale flowed, our worries faded away. I loved these nights. Even though we knew war was coming, the togetherness was overwhelming. I was sure that if Heggalund were to walk in right now, he would die instantly; struck down by the sheer joy and compassion that filled the great hall.

Erik was staring at Manara with drunken eyes, and as he raised his ale to his lips, I asked;

'Have you humped her yet.'

His ale sprayed across the table and everyone laughed except Guthrom, who was sitting directly opposite.

'Well, have you?' I repeated.

'I have. Why are you jealous? Rognvaldr not as good as you hoped?'

'He's good… really good and no, I'm not jealous.'

'Then we are both lucky and should celebrate our good fortune.' He filled my drinking vessel, and we clashed them together.

'Skol,' he shouted, and I echoed the toast.

Tonight, we were happy, and regardless of the thoughts of my peers; I had decided that tomorrow I would execute my plan and pray Heggalund would bring his army to kill me.

CHAPTER TWENTY-FIVE

The following morning, after my sword practice with Guthrom, I went in search of Finnulf. I needed his help to set my trap.

There were so many people in Hundrop now, that finding one individual was a challenge. I found Cinead first, who was far from sober and of no use to me what so ever. He picked me up and squeezed me like a bear, expelling every piece of air from my young lungs, my ribs threatening to snap at any moment.

'Finnulf?' I gasped as Cinead released his grip. 'Where's Finnulf?' I repeated.

'He was here a moment ago; had a young wench with him but they both seemed to have disappeared now,' he burped then farted, which amused him. I raised my eyes to the heavens and continued my search. The streets were packed with warriors. Some were sharpening swords and axes while others, half naked, exited huts with smiles as wide as the river that passed nearby.

Trying to find one person in a throng of nine hundred was proving difficult.

As I turned a corner and made towards the main gate, I saw a few of the men that had fought with us against Oddvar.

'Have you seen Finnulf?' I asked.

'Your too late Helga, he has taken a woman already.'

They chortled, believing themselves amusing until they saw my blazing green eyes and stern expression.

'Finnulf?' I repeated.

'He's over there,' one pointed. 'In the boat, with a girl.'

I made towards the small Karve that was rocking gently in the river's current. Finnulf was rocking gently also, his bare arse embedded between the thighs of a buxom wench and his head nestled between her ample breasts.

'Finnulf, I need you,' I shouted, which was probably the wrong thing to say at that moment.

'Get in the queue,' was the reply.

'Finnulf,' I yelped.

'Helga, can't it wait?' he complained.

'No, I need your help,' He ignored me and quickened his stroke.

'Finnulf,' I screamed, losing my patience and trying to ignore the moans and groans of their humping.

'Let me finish for Odin's sake.' He begged.

'Be quick.' I snapped.

'He's never anything else,' the woman barked which made Finnulf give up, much to my amusement.

As we walked up the riverbank and back towards the centre of the village, I whispered, not wanting to be overheard.

'You told me you had skills, that you can blend in, be

unseen.'

'What of it,' he asked.

'I want you to leave now and infiltrate Heggalund's camp.' He stopped walking and stared at me.

'Are you serious?' he questioned, eyes glaring and mouth ajar.

'Deadly serious, can you do it or not?' I knew it was an enormous thing to ask. I was asking Finnulf to risk his life for someone he had only just met. 'Well, can you?'

He considered it for a moment before answering. 'I can, but why? What is there to gain?'

'Everything. Now listen carefully, this is what I want you to do. Take a horse and travel back to where we fought Oddvar. The bodies will still be there. Find a shield and any other items you need to persuade Heggalund that you are one of Oddvar's men. Once you gain an audience, tell him we let you live so you could deliver a message to him; got that?' He nodded, so I continued. 'Let him know you faced an army of women, mad women, like berserkers, three hundred in total with swords, spears and bows. We fought like Valkyries, slaughtering all before us and denying any entry to Odin's hall.' I paused while Finnulf repeated what I had just said, then continued.

'Good, then inform him that a pale-faced girl with red flamed hair led them. Her name is Helga.'

'That's you,' he blurted.

'I know it is. Pay attention. Finally, and don't forget this bit Finnulf; tell him that he killed my mother near a stone circle on an island to the west, and that I have come here to take my revenge. Let him know that I will wait with my three hundred warriors in the valley till the sun is at its highest. If he fails to show, then I will tell everyone in every kingdom that Heggalund fears me. Don't elaborate, just say it as I just did.' He nodded, but I could tell he was uneasy. I placed my hands gently on his shoulders.

'Finnulf, I know I'm asking a lot of you, but this has to work. We you do this?'

'I will, but if I succeed, you will owe me.'

'Fine; if we survive, we can discuss that, now go deliver the message, then get out of there and ride South to find my father. Explain to him my plan and urge him to make haste, for my life depends upon his timely arrival.' I hugged him tight, and he hugged me back.

'Stay safe, may Thor protect you.'

Finnulf said nothing more; he just left quickly. I waited a while until I saw him leave through the gates of Hundorp, everything now depended upon his success.

'Where have you been? And where is Finnulf going in such a hurry?' Rognvaldr was drunk, I could tell as he staggered towards me.

'He's gone to ask Odin for help,' I lied, putting a steadying arm around my lover's waste.

'Well, let's hope he comes and brings his sons with him. For it will take all of Thor's strength and most of Loki's trickery to bring us victory.' I kissed him gently and stroked his face. The smell of ale tinged his breath, but I didn't care.

CHAPTER TWENTY-SIX

That night I struggled to sleep, unlike Rognvaldr, whose snoring kept me awake as much as my anxiety. The day had passed without incident and our scouts had returned to inform us that there was no movement in the valley. I feared Finnulf had failed in his mission and that I may have sent him to his death.

It was just breaking light once more; so I gave up on any thought of slumber and dragged myself out of our bed. I felt weary, but a bucket of icy water splashed over my face, hastily sharpened my senses. I dressed quickly, and walked out into the cool morning air, hopeful of finding someone to share my fears with.

As I wandered through the huts and dwellings, a large dog barked at my passing. I shushed it, not wanting to disturb those who were sleeping. I was not alone outside. Many men and women were already up and about. Some, like me, looked as if they too had been robbed of sleep. They nodded as I passed, but no one spoke. There was no need, for we were all dealing with our own internal thoughts and weaknesses, and this was not the time to share with others. Our silence was our strength.

I was relieved when I saw Cinead. A friendly face was exactly what I needed, and they didn't come friendlier than his. He was sitting sharpening his sword with a grinding stone, and was so concentrated on the sharpness of his blade that he failed to acknowledge my approach.

'You're up early.' My sudden arrival made him jump.

'You shouldn't creep up on me like that, especially whilst I'm working on my blade.' He frowned, but that was the limit of his ire.

'Sorry Cinead, I will throw something at you next time to get your attention.' He ignored me and continued his sharpening.

'Where are the others?' I asked.

'Guthrom is with Hakon and Erik is where he always is now.'

'With Manara,' I interjected. Cinead nodded before adding.

'His cock must be red raw, he's infatuated by her,' I laughed and Cinead's frown dispersed as he laughed too.

'Your just jealous,' I suggested and Cinead shrugged.

'Maybe I am. It has been so long since a woman shared my bed, I forget what it's like.' I had never thought of Cinead as having the same needs as other men. He had always been my guide and teacher. My port in a storm and a fellow outsider. We had always been close since the moment he jumped into the sea to save me all those years ago. He too had heard my mother's voice beneath the waves, and that connection had stayed with us. I loved him dearly. He was the rock that I clung to when the storm was at its fiercest.

'You have never spoken to me of this before. Why now?'

He turned to face me, his round cheeks framed by his slightly greying hair.

'I worry that time is running out Helga, that this maybe my last battle. The odds are against us, and if Harald doesn't come in time…'

I grabbed his face in my hands and squeezed his apple shaped cheeks between my fingers and thumbs.

'He will come, and when he does, the wrath of the Gods will rain down on our enemies. We will tear them apart and feed them to the ravens. Now is not the time for us to lose faith. We will win. Even now, whilst we sit here together, Heggalund is being coerced to come west through the valley. He is falling into my trap, and once in it, there will be no escape and no mercy. He is the fly that lands on the spider's web, stuck with nowhere to go, waiting for the inevitable arrival of the spider, and when that spider comes he dies.' I kissed his forehead and smiled.

'You have such a way with words, I almost believe you,' he said as he edged his blade once more.

'Finish that later,' I whispered. 'I need you to help me find three hundred women that look like they could fight. Come on,' I urged.

On the way, I told Cinead what I had done, and he could not believe it.

'Guthrom is right about you, I should have left you in the sea when I had the chance. You've gone too far this time, Helga. you had no right to take things into your own hands.'

I didn't care what Eystein and Hakon thought. I just hoped Finnulf had delivered my message, and that Heggalund had fallen for the ruse. If he had; then he was coming to Gaulardal, with all his men, to wipe away the child that had cursed him all those years ago, and to take Hundorp and its kingdom.

It was light now, and the village was coming alive. People were going about their business as if nothing much had changed. Boats left to fish the river, whilst women prepared a morning meal. Children pretended to be warriors with wooden swords and shields, as I had done in Vestfold. It seemed so normal, but a hoard was gathering in the East, and if they came, nothing would ever be the same again. This battle would change everything.

We found Manara and Erik in the barn, still sleeping, wrapped together under a woolen blanket. They woke as the light from the open door streamed over their faces. They squinted as I yelled at them to dress and come with us. Cinead blushed as Manara leapt up, unabashed by her nakedness. He stared for a while until I punched his arm and pulled him outside.

There were many women in Hundorp but most were not warrior material, however we found some that could hold a sword and shield and looked convincing enough to fight.

'They just have to look the part, Erik. They are just bait.' I explained. Erik didn't really get it, even though he pretended he did. Cinead laughed and whispered at me:

'Too much of a good thing. Manara has weakened his brain.'

'Let's hope he has kept his fighting skills.' Manara shot me a glance that told me she had heard us; she was not best pleased.

'I would like to come along as part of your army, Helga, if you believe that I am not weakened by my humping,' I smiled at her sarcastic tone.

'You were first on my list, now how many have we got?' Cinead did a quick count as Guthrom arrived with Hakon and Eystein.

'Two hundred, maybe a few more.' Eystein glanced at the women.

'What's this?' he flicked a finger at the group and seemed irritated. I took a deep breath before explaining.

'My Lord, I told you I could get Heggalund to come through the valley, well these women will help me do it.' I quickly explained what I had done and Finnulf's part in it. Hakon laughed and Guthrom just stared at me. However, Eystein was not so impressed.

'This will never work; your foolishness will get us all killed.' He continued ranting at me as I stood, ignoring most of what he said. When he had finished, I replied:

'It's too late, it's done, and if my plan has worked, then they are on their way. If not, then they are going south, so what difference does it make, my Lord? You had all night to come up with something and you come up with nothing. I have at least tried.' I bowed ironically and smiled petulantly.

'Helga a word.' Guthrom motioned me to one side, and I could tell he was not best pleased by my behaviour.

'You need to be more respectful and less arrogant.' I tried to say something, but Guthrom cut me off. 'Listen Helga, for once in your life. Take notice. Eystein is the King of this district, so show him some respect. You are not his equal. He has tolerated you for now because Åseda and Rognvaldr are fond of you, but you need to stop antagonizing him. Others would have been less tolerant. Your plan has merit, but your application of it without consulting with the rest of us was a mistake.'

'I tried Guthrom but nobody would listen, I make my own decisions and I stand by them, what's done is done.'

I stayed quiet while the others discussed what I had done. As expected, Eystein did not like it, describing it as immature and something that a warrior like Heggalund would never fall for. It was Åseda that spoke up in my defence.

'Helga has been brave, although impetuous, she has acted in good faith. I for one believe in her. If Heggalund thinks that women defeated Oddar and his men, how can he just turn away from that and pretend it didn't happen. His curiosity will make him want to see these warriors for himself, and to be on the safe side, he may bring all his men just to show his invincibility, a show of his strength so to speak. For one so young, Helga has great insight into the minds of men, and I think she may be right, so we should prepare for his arrival. I too will stand with Helga in her shield wall.' Aseda looked at her husband, daring him to argue the point. She was so like Asa; as I had witnessed her sister do the same thing to my father. Woman had more power over their men, than their men were willing to admit.

Hakon threw an arm around my shoulder.
'I agree with my daughter, Eystein. We should let this play out. After all, what have we got to lose. Give Helga her women and throw a hundred of my warriors in for good measure. He is more likely to believe her tale if men also stand in her ranks. What do you say Guthrom?'

'I agree, we don't really have any other option now. Let's just hope Finnulf brings Harald before they overrun us. If he does, then we will stand a chance.'

Guthrom looked at me. He looked jaded and unsure, and I realized that in that moment, he was doubtful it would work, but he was willing to stand by me regardless, to see it through to the bitter end.

'He will come. I am sure of it, and when he does, I will lure him in. By the time he realises what's happening, it will be too late.' As always, I exuded confidence; but internally I was far less assured, verging on the edge of panic.

'My Lord Eystein,' I turned to the king, lowering my head in respect.

'I was wrong to act without your knowledge and consent. I have no excuse for that. The Queen is right, I am young, headstrong and driven by the need to avenge my mother's death. It gets the better of me at times and I am sorry for that.' I caught myself twirling my hair between my fingers and thumb, a habit I had as a young child, a nervous trait when I had been naughty or had done wrong. How strange I should revert to such behaviour here, I thought. 'However, I am willing to give my life in the defence of your kingdom, but I don't feel that today is my dying day. I believe the Gods will help us earn a glorious victory and the Skalds will tell stories and sing songs to remind future generations of this day. The day that King Glumra and Jarl Grjotgardsson led their warriors and defeated a mighty giant in the bowels of Gaulardal.'

Hakon smiled.

'I like the thought of that, don't you, Eystein?' he said.

Eystein had no choice but to agree. He had been in an impossible position from the very beginning, and now his fate laid in the hands of a girl seventeen summers old.

'I suppose I do,' he acknowledged.

Everyone cheered, and those carrying swords raised them to the heavens.

It was time to go to war.

CHAPTER TWENTY-SEVEN

With Hakon's warriors intermingled with the woman we had mustered; we almost had the three hundred I needed to face Heggalund. We practiced hard, forming a shield wall as quickly and efficiently as we could; it had to look convincing, and on the whole it did, although a few struggled and were removed by Guthrom and sent home.

'Not too bad,' he commended. 'Now let's hear you roar.'

The women screamed, and everyone laughed.

'You sound like a flock of seagulls,' he mused. 'Maybe you could fly above them and shit on their heads.' Even Eystein smiled, but the approach of riders stilled their mirth.

The group was galloping with pace and urgency; we recognized them as Hakon's men, and as they pulled up beside us; I moved closer to hear their news.

'My Lord the army marches, they are coming west through Gaulardal.'

'All of them?' Eystein enquired.

'All of them my Lord.' In that moment I thought of Finnulf. He had risked so much for me and I hoped he had made it out safely, and was now with my father.

'Well, Helga looks like the first part of your strategy has worked. You had better get your women ready.' Hakon placed a calming hand on my shoulder, sensing my excitement.

'Stay calm, clear in thought, don't let your emotions rule your head. Stick to the plan, Helga.'

'Don't worry grandfather, I will.'

The others were still practicing as I approached. My wide smile and exuberance excluded the need for words.

'They are coming then?' Said Erik calmly.

'Yes, they are coming. We should leave now; I need to get Thunder. Manara, fetch Cloud, we must go. Shit, where did I put my sword.'

Two enormous hands grabbed my shoulders from behind, spinning me round. It was Cinead.

'Stop, we have plenty of time. I will prepare your horse and ready your things. You have other matters to attend to.' He pointed to Rognvaldr, who was standing with his father and brother but looking in my direction. I had forgotten all about him and now felt guilty, realising that we may never see each other again if things went wrong. I cussed myself for being so selfish and allowing my thoughts to spin in turmoil. I moved toward him and grabbing his hand pulled him away.

Our lovemaking was torrid and unlike the times before. I bit and scratched as he forcibly spread my thighs and penetrated me. There was no kissing or caressing, there was just urgency, as if time was running out. It was soon over, but the act had soothed my brain and swelled my heart.

'I love you,' I whispered in his ear and he held me close,

pushing one more time, enjoying the moment.

As we gathered ourselves, I felt awkward and believed Rognvaldr felt the same. I, for one, felt embarrassed. By allowing my feelings to be expressed with words made me feel weak, almost womanly, yet I wanted so much for him to reciprocate.

'I will look for you in battle,' he stuttered. He could not look at me.

'I would be honoured to fight by your side, but I do not need your protection.' My words were petulant and as I gathered my things and left, he caught my arm.

'Helga.' I turned to face him. His head was lowered and his eyes looked upwards. He looked like a scolded puppy.

'That was not what I meant. I want to be by your side, in peace and in battle. If we survive this, will you be my woman?'

In the heat of passion I had voiced my affection and he had stayed silent, my heart so wanted to say yes but today was not the day to talk of such things, I had waited so long for this, so my reply was short shrift.

'I will be your lover if that's what you mean, but anything more; well we will have to wait and see how the day unfolds. We may both be dining with Odin by nightfall.' I pulled away and left without looking back, even though I was desperate, too.

Thunder was waiting for me, dressed for battle. I patted the side of his face and he stamped a foot with excitement. Cinead gave me a hand up, and I could tell he was worried. I bent down and kissed the top of his head; he looked up and his eyes betrayed his fear.

'You must prevail, Eithne,' he said, using my birth name. 'I could not bear to lose you. I love you like my own and I will be there when you need me.' He grabbed my hand and squeezed it like you would a child.

'You have always been there Cinead, I love you too.' I pulled on the reins and trotted off, looking over my shoulder at the man who had rescued me from the cold northern sea all those summers ago. He had taught me so much, but now it was time for me to fulfil my destiny.

Erik and Manara were waiting with the others. Guthrom was there, too

'One more time,' he barked, and my troops overlapped their shields once more. 'That's more like it,' he said, nodding appreciatively.

'It's time we left.' I wanted to get moving. My skin crawled and tingled as my nerves were trying to get the better of me. My mouth was dry, and I struggled to swallow. If I felt like this now, how would I feel when I was facing two thousand warriors. I pushed that thought quickly away.

'You coming with us Guthrom?' I asked.

'No Helga, Cinead and I will be with Hakon. I trust you to behave yourself and follow the plan. After all, it was your idea.'

He stared at me expressionless, but the slight twitch in his lip betrayed his genuine feelings. I had hated this man, as he believed me wild, untameable, and selfish. Yet now I realised that he had been right all along, but thanks to his training and guidance, I had changed, if only slightly.

'I will miss you in the shield wall Guthrom.' His lips cracked a smile.

'Next time, Helga, there's always a next time. Oh, and before you leave, I have something for you.' He waved his arm and a woman he had removed from the ranks brought out a banner. It flapped in the breeze, but a black wolf could be seen clearly on the triangular fabric. It reminded me of Gunnolf.

'Why the Wolf?' I asked.

'They are intelligent, you're not. I pray Odin will see it and gift you some of their attributes. You might just survive the day if he does.' He handed it to me as I laughed.

'Thank you, I will treasure it.'

'Make sure you do and keep it close. It will help me find

you.' I nodded, realizing that every one of my dearest friends had sworn to find me this day and that brought me great comfort. I had lived my young life in their company, being a nuisance, not conforming, always wanting to fight. I had put them at risk several times because of my beliefs and selfishness, yet still they wished to stand with me, protect me as they had always done, and die by my side if needs must.

I was blessed to have such a family.

CHAPTER TWENTY-EIGHT

In my dreams, I had imagined this day so many times. Cold and wet, a mud-filled battlefield of broken bodies and headless corpses. With sword and shield and a roar of anger coursing through my veins, I would charge forward and reap my revenge on Heggalund. Yet, as we left Hundorp, the sun blazed high in a cloudless sky. A hawk hovered, searching for prey, and larks sang a tuneful accord. It shattered my dreams. I was fearful that the Gods had abandoned me and that my dreams were one of hope, not truth. I thought of my mother dying at the hands of my enemy, and it pierced my heart. I never knew what happened to my father, but the memory of the smoking village and the flames that flickered in the night sky did not bode well. He was gone from my life and, whether alive or dead, he no longer played a part in it. Then my thoughts turned to Groa and wished I had never started the journey that had led to her cave. Unwittingly, I had caused her death, a terrible and cruel demise that she definitely did not deserve. I kept her secret and as I glanced at Erik; I could see his resemblance to the mother he never knew. *'The Gods can be fickle,'* she had said, and she was right, for as we reached the narrow entrance to Gaulardal there was no sign of an army and my heart sank.

We waited; there was nothing else we could do. Eystein's scouts had said they were coming, yet so far, their presence was non-existent. Erik took a handful of men and ventured into the valley. I watched as they climbed a peak that would give them an excellent view of the entire valley. They were soon too small to make out, so I dismounted Thunder and sat on the sun-baked grass. Manara climbed down from Cloud and joined me.

'Don't fret Helga, they will come. I can feel it.'

'I don't know. This feels all wrong. I was so sure of myself, certain that Heggalund would not resist my taunting, but on reflection, why should he come, I am nobody. He is a Jarl with a massive army that wants kingdoms and power. What am I compared to that?'

'You are Harald Harfagre's daughter, and you have challenged him and his authority. So he must come. He probably fears you and wonders if the Gods are in fact on your side. He's late because he's looking for omens, signs from his Gods that all is well. However, there is no sign, so he's waiting a bit longer, but eventually he will have to come.' Her words made sense, and Groa had said to trust in the Gods. I stood and walked towards Thunder, plucking my shield and banner from its harness. I drew my sword and sauntered into the Valley, Manara and the others followed. The ground was hard and stone filled, but I found a small grassy area that would yield enough for my banner to stand. It fluttered in the quirky breeze.

'He wants a sign? Let's give him one.'

I ordered a shield wall and laughed manically as it formed effortlessly. Guthrom's training had paid off. Then, together and in rhythm, we banged our swords onto our shields as hard as we could. The mountainous valley reverberated and echoed, amplifying our battle cry. The sound was immense. Within moments, I saw Erik and the others coming toward us. I knew then that they were coming.

I was not prepared for their arrival. They looked like ants scuttling upon the valley floor, but the dust that billowed signalled that these were far bigger and much harder to kill.

Some women gasped and shuffled their feet as if to run.

'Stand still,' I screamed. 'If you run, they will hunt you down and slaughter you. They will rape your daughters and kill your sons. They will show you no mercy, and I would rather die here with you than live under their tyranny. We stand here together for Hundorp, Vestfold and all the Kingdoms in between.' The shuffling stopped, and I turned again to face the marching ants. I wanted to run too.

A warrior rushed from the ranks and yelled in my ear that

our forces were in position. I looked back but could see nothing beyond the narrowing. I felt isolated, fearful, and terrified. My body shook, so I gripped my sword and shield harder until it hurt. Erik moved close,

'This will be fun,' he whispered. I looked at him and he was grinning insanely. I couldn't speak, my tongue was so dry in my mouth that I couldn't form words.

'When this starts, remember your training. Keep moving, use your speed and agility to kill or maim, then move on. I will be right beside you. Thor is with us.'

Erik always knew what to say, even though his mind was not his strongest muscle. The mention of Thor calmed me. The shakes slowed, then finally ceased as my self-control returned as if by magic. Turning my attention back to the approaching forces, I noticed how quickly they had advanced. I could make out faces now. Men with long beards and tattooed faces, clad in leather or mail. Most with swords or axes, but some had bows, and it was them I feared the most. A silent killer too swift to deflect.

'They're in a hurry,' my voice cracked.

'They will stop soon and throw insults. Heggalund will want to speak with you before he kills you, I'm sure.' Erik was eerily calm, a veteran warrior who did not fear death. He was so self-assured, knowing that his seat was waiting for him in Valhalla. I was not so sure that Odin would be so willing to take a whelp of a woman who dared to enter the realm of men.

Erik was right. The army stopped just beyond the range of bows. I could hear heckles and taunts, but the breeze that caressed my ears dulled them. However, as six men moved forward, I heard my name and there was Heggalund, arms spread wide, smiling through his grey tinged beard, no sword or shield, just confidence. I turned to Erik and Manara.

'Will you come?' I asked.

'Wouldn't miss it for the world,' Erik replied.

'Where Erik goes I go,' said Manara. Which made me smile, and question if I had been too hard on Rognvaldr.

I felt so weak; and was totally out of my depth. I now had skills with a sword and shield, but compared to these men, I was a novice. Erik, always empathic, could see my doubt and felt my anguish.

'Helga,' he said calmly. 'Look at those men standing there before us.' I looked and could see their contempt, sneering and mocking, knowing that they would slaughter us, or worse. I watched as some displayed their cocks, hardening themselves and shouting obscenities in my direction. Heggalund was laughing and grabbed himself as his warriors cheered.

'Now remember what they did to your mother, your father, and your village. Each is responsible for her death. By allegiance, they follow the man who took her life, raped her and removed her head. Remember that Helga, allow it to build your anger and give you strength. You have an army, now you must lead it. It's time to let the monster out.'

 I looked at Erik. Gone was the simple man who struggled with his words and sometimes lacked intelligence. Instead, there was a warrior, battle hardened, who would stand with me until the end. I knew Erik would give his life for me. He had offered it before. His words stirred me, memories flashed back, and I felt my anger rise in the pit of my stomach. I rose slowly at first, but soon gathered momentum. It kissed my heart as it travelled through my throat and finally expelled itself in my voice.

'Follow me,' I growled.

I counted the steps, eighty-two, an insignificant amount but enough to put me within striking distance of the man I hated so much. I was tempted, but I had made a promise to stick to the plan and so I resisted the urge.

Heggalund spoke first.

'So this is the girl Harald took from me all those summers ago. Nice enough face and a fine body, skinny, but I'm sure I could fatten you up.' His men laughed, and I smiled.

'Jarl Heggalund, still trying to be a king, I see.' His lip twitched slightly, enough to say I had touched a nerve.

'Spirit too, I like that in a girl.' He emphasized the girl, hoping it would annoy, but it didn't, only Guthrom could get that kind of reaction from me.

'Is this your army, Helga?'

'It is yes. Are you impressed?'

Laughing, he turned to his men.

'Are we impressed?' he shouted.

His men jeered and shouted their contempt, banging their swords and axes on shields once more. As the noise died down, Heggalund added.

'I guess not.'

At that moment, I noticed a chill. It ran its fingers up my back and whispered in my ear. I looked around and saw black clouds forming. The wind had picked up, and it played with my hair. I took a step toward Heggalund and pointed my sword at his throat. His men stepped forward, but he raised a hand to stop them.

'You think my army small, but we have a God on our side. Look,' I pointed at the black mass that was gathering behind us.

'He's coming, hammer in hand, to help me strike you down. I will kill you, gut you, slice you open and feed you to my wolf. He is here too, watching you from the hills, preparing for his feast.' His demeanour changed. He tried to stare me down, but his eyes had noticed the clouds gathering and they flicked from side to side in search of Gunnolf. I stepped back, turned my back and walked back toward my shields and Wolf banner. It blew proudly in the darkening sky, and I laughed as the first rumbles of thunder cracked through Gaulardal.

'Thor is here,' I screamed, and my women cheered, pointing their swords skyward.

CHAPTER TWENTY-NINE

I looked up as the first droplets of rain fell. They were cold and stung my face, but I was glad to see them. If omens existed, then this surely was one. I was no longer shaking; I felt calm, exhilarated, yearning to fight. Thor was with me, and as I looked at the enemy, something caught my eye. For a fleeting moment, I thought I saw Groa standing with Gunnolf in the far distance behind Heggalund's army. But when I looked again, they were gone, replaced instead by a stony crag that decorated the valley wall. I put it down to a trick of the light, but I prayed that what I had seen was real, and that she was here to see me take revenge for those I had loved and lost.

Then the arrows flew.

'Shields,' Erik shouted.

I looked skyward, and that almost got me killed. It was hypnotic, an angry mass of wood and feather arching across rain-filled clouds.

'Helga,' came the scream, and I reacted just in time as the storm of arrows peppered our shields. Screams followed, echoing through the valley. I turned to look and noticed that some had fallen, whilst others crawled away injured and wailing. Another volley followed, and we all hankered down again behind our shields, waiting for the impact. There were fewer screams this time, which was a blessing, but there were still injuries and several dead.

Then they came. They were in no rush and I watched as they casually walked towards us; they had stung us with their arrows and now they were coming to slaughter.

'We need to move… now.' I shouted, and our people did not need telling twice. There was no time to help the injured that couldn't walk. Seeing our retreat, Heggalund had urged his men forward, and now they ran. Many pleaded and begged us for help; but if we had stayed, we would all have fallen and lost any chance of a victory. So as the heavens opened, we ran, as planned, and thankfully Heggalund followed.

The ground was so sloppy now, and several were stumbling as we raced towards the narrow entrance where our army waited. There was no time to look back, but you could sense our predators behind us. They were closing in for the kill, but they too struggled on the now sodden ground.

The rain was so heavy now, as pebble like droplets pooled in the troughs and hollows of the valley floor. It was quickly turning into a quagmire. I was breathless, my lungs pained as fear and the exertion of running removed all the air and moisture from within them. My throat burned like the sword maker's furnace, and although the air was cold and damp, I was sweating profusely. It seemed to take an age to reach our haven, but reach it we did, and as we passed through the gap, our comrades formed a shield wall behind us. I stopped and turned just in time to see the first row of Heggalund's army strike against our barrier. Several of his men had hesitated upon seeing that we were not alone, but the ones behind, eager to fight, had pushed them onwards, skewering them onto the waiting spears.

Death is never easy to watch, even if it is an enemy. As I regained my breath, I watched the pushing and shoving off the shield wall. I saw men die with horrific injuries; one whose head was hanging to one side was still standing as if unwilling to die. As the shield wall heaved, it threw him to one side where he fell, blood gushing from his split throat. His eyes stared at me as if pleading, begging. I knew he was dead, and that this was the brutality of war. In truth, I was ill prepared.

'Helga, are you all right?'

Recognizing Guthrom's voice, I almost collapsed into his arms. Shaking, not through fear, but with relief, I hugged him tightly.

Guthrom reciprocated my hug and stroked my hair. It was a

strange moment in the heat of battle, but his touch helped regain my composure and I felt safe with him by my side.

'It worked,' I gasped.

'It did yes, but now they are here we have to fight hard and hold on until your father hopefully arrives.'

Time does not exist in battle, and there is no place for tiredness or fatigue. With so many people in one place, it was hard to distinguish who is a friend and who is the enemy. Guthrom had told me once, '*if they are coming at you with a sword in hand, kill them and ask them later if they meant you harm.*' I had laughed when he had said this, but now I totally understood. Battle is total chaos.

I had started at the back of the wall, which was deep and still holding back the hoard that pressed forward against us. However, as things progressed, I had somehow made my way closer to the front.

There was a smell of shit and piss, ale filled breath and the putridness of death. Slipping, I fell into a warm stream of blood and internal organs, and vomited immediately. I spat it sideways as hands lifted me up; With every heave, I was pushed forward once more, ever closer to the front.

Like a viper, writhing and bending, the wall pulsed forward, then back; the enemy tried to break us, but we held firm. Men were tiring and slight gaps were appearing. I feared we would buckle and If we did, it would be a slaughter. Men rushed to plug the gaps, but it was only a temporary fix.

I saw Rognvaldr; he stood with his brother Sigurd in the front row and I could see the strain and effort they both applied to keep the wall intact. His eyes bulged with the effort, and every vein stood prominently upon his neck. There was bruising on his face, probably caused by a shield boss, and blood ran from his lips. I observed all this in a matter of moments, as I attempted to push my way through the throng to be with him. If I was to die, then I would do it by his side.

He saw me and I saw his concern; but I was there now, so there was little he could do about it. Some of his men saw me too, those in the second row who supported the front and filled the gaps when men fell. I joined them and pushed with all the effort I could muster. Sigurd laughed,

'Push men, show this moon mad bitch how men fight.' He shouted.

Squeezed between sweat-covered monsters, I pushed even harder. They were giants compared to me, but I played my part in responding to Sigurd's call. Like gods, we streamed forward over the dead and dying, stamping and stabbing if we considered them to be an enemy. Their shield wall broke, and normally when this occurred, you would take advantage. But we were not there to break them; we were there to hold them, so we resisted the temptation. They did not plug the gap and were stepping back.

'Hold the line; do not follow,' It sounded like Eystein, but I could not see his face among so many. We held the line, shield-lapping shield, but our enemy was retreating slowly, step-by-step. They still faced us and many gestured for us to follow, but we resisted, mostly. The odd warrior drunk with the battle lust did race forward inviting death. They were immediately cut down, holding on tight to their weapons as they crumpled in the red stained mud.

Still, the enemy moved back, revealing mounds of bodies that had fallen in the narrow opening of Gaulardal. There were so many, their blood had stained the grass and even the rain failed to cleanse it. Instead, small crimson rivulets trickled through the stalks and leaves and collected in pools around the mass of corpses. It was as if the clouds had cried tears of blood.

Sigurd suddenly stepped forward from the wall.

'What are you doing, brother?' screamed Rognvaldr.

'Listen, can't you hear it?'

I heard nothing. A shield wall is not the quietest of places, even when the battle had ceased.

'There you hear it?' Sigurd shouted once more, as we watched the enemy amble away. Several of them were looking away from us, as if they feared a demon lurking behind them.

It was then we heard the roar and a clash of shields.

'Father,' I whispered. Then I screamed out loud.

'Guthrom, my father has come.'

I don't know if Guthrom heard me, but others did, and word spread fast throughout our lines. A roar sounded and men pushed from the back, forcing us through the gap like ale from a jug. I looked at Rognvaldr and shouted,

'Let's finish them.'

CHAPTER THIRTY

Gaulardal was overflowing with the sounds of combat. Shield walls had disintegrated now as I swiftly walked through the bodies of the fallen. No more pushing or shoving. This was hand-to-hand now, and I revelled in it. Rognvaldr and Sigurd were with me when we were rushed by a small group of men. I counted six, two each, I thought, but three ran towards me, sensing a quick and easy kill.

Guthrom had trained me well for this kind of situation.

'Keep moving,' he had said. 'You can use your shield for defence and attack. It is a weapon and hurts like hell when smashed into your opponent's face. Use it to deflect and push away when faced by several attackers.'

I scanned the three quickly and had determined my biggest threat. He carried a battle-axe but no shield, and with two hands and from a distance, he attempted to hook my shield away from my body so his comrades could move in close and stab at me with their swords. I was more than ready, and as the axe connected with my shield, I knew I had to dispatch him quickly. Speed was my best weapon and as the axe lipped onto my shield, I raced forward. Pushing my shield against its handle, I drove the head skyward. His protectors were too slow to respond and with no shield to protect him, I drove my sword into his gut and pushed him backwards until he fell. It was not a fatal blow, but it incapacitated him and he would die from the wound, eventually. There was no time to finish him as another raced to his aid. A sword slashed towards my throat, but I blocked it easily. I parried, using both sword and shield, until an opportunity arrived. I feigned an opening, and he took the bait. It was a risk, but it worked. I opened my defence just enough to allow him to strike at my midriff. He was quick, and I glimpsed a smile of satisfaction, thinking he had gained the upper hand; but as he surged forward to skewer me, I just turned sideways, narrowly avoiding the point of his sword. I slammed my shield into him as hard as I could, bringing it up and outwards. With more luck than intent, the edge connected with his chin and his head shot backwards as his legs slipped from beneath him. As he hit the deck, I skewered him. I had used so much effort in my kill that my sword had become imbedded in the ground below his twitching corpse. Blood pumped from his wound with each dying heartbeat. It soaked my hand and sword handle, making it hard to grasp, and before I had the time to regain a grip, the third warrior was on me. There was no skill or elegance in his attack. His attention was just to beat me down. He carried a shorter handled axe and was hammering it into my shield. I had only just managed to raise it before his onslaught. Forced backwards, I scrambled away, whilst being beaten and pummeled. I had lost my sword and grabbed for my dagger. Still he came forward, hammering blows into my disintegrating shield. There was no escape, and I waited for death.

A silent killer, a goose-feathered assassin brought relief from the onslaught and saved me.

He fell forward and coughed a mixture of spittle and blood onto my face. As I wiped it away and pushed him off me, I noticed Manara, bow in hand. Erik raced towards me and pulled me upright. He retrieved my sword, wiping it on his tunic before handing it back to me.

'Don't lose it again,' he barked, his eyes wild and angry looking. I just nodded and approached Manara, who reached down and lifted my Wolf banner from the sludge of battle.

'Help me find Heggalund,' I shouted. Trying to make my girlish voice heard over the noise of battle.

So the three of us moved on, deeper into the valley, each of us protecting one another. I was glad Erik and Manara were by my side, as I had lost Rognvaldr and Sigurd during my previous encounter.

The valley was overflowing with warriors; some fought alone while others banded together in small groups. It was savage, cruel, and as my eyes scanned the masses looking for Heggalund, we were attacked once more.

There was no time for Manara to nock an arrow, so she unhitched her shield and drew her small sword, planting the wolf banner deep into the sodden ground. It flapped in the rain-swept breeze as we rallied beside it. I found a shield on the ground and raised it in preparation. Standing with Erik and Manara, I waited for our enemy.

Our opponents laughed and spat insults as they approached and I watched and waited, not noticing that others had joined us. Soon our numbers had swelled and the men that faced us charged. Once more, the sounds of wood and steel thudded in the damp air as one side tried to gain the advantage. Spears were thrust and axes swung, each hoping to connect.

We separated, picking a target to attack. I picked the biggest target I could find, hoping he would be slow and cumbersome, giving me the advantage of agility over brute strength.

That was my first mistake, for this was no ordinary warrior. Racing forward, I attacked and was swatted aside like an annoying fly. The power in the shield blow winded me badly as I fell backwards. I couldn't breathe and felt on the verge of unconsciousness. My vision was blurred and the pain inside my body was severe. I figured ribs were broken, but knew if I stayed down, I would surely die. A howl of delight rang out, and the fog cleared. The troll was standing growling at me and biting the edge of his shield like a madman. I tried to stand, but he kicked me back down, his boot filling my face and smashing my nose. I had lost my shield but held on tight to my sword, hoping it would get me into Freya's hall at least. Pathetically, I held it out, trying to defend myself, waiting for death to come. It was then I heard Guthrom's voice

'There is no honour in killing a woman. Kill me instead.' He roared.

Manara ran to my aid, helping to my feet. I watched as Guthrom attacked the monster. I could see his delight at being back where he felt he belonged. Age left him, as his sword sang of long-forgotten battles and untold victories.

My head and face pulsed, and every inhalation brought a searing pain to my side, shortening my breath to gasps as I staggered upright.

'Manara, my shield,' I squeaked, hardly able to talk.

'You need to withdraw your injured.' I said nothing as I pushed her aside and attempted to retrieve my shield. Grimacing, I bent down, picking up the battered circle of wood and leather. I was hurt, but I would not withdraw, not until I found Heggalund.

Guthrom blocked each killing blow that reigned in, laughing at his assailant, mocking him as he sidestepped and parried. Then, without warning, he struck. I watched as the lumbering ox closed on Guthrom, covering the gap between them swiftly. Yet my teacher made him look slow. As he swung his sword, Guthrom blocked it with ease, pushing it to one side whist at the same time striking with his own. The tip of his sword sliced his opponent's throat before he had any chance of raising his shield. It was more of a flick than a stab, and I watched as a split appeared, running red across his neck. Eyes bulging and eerily silent, he dropped to his knees as the first stream of blood gushed from the wound. Guthrom was not finished yet and smiling, he bent low and spat into the dying man's face.

'Helga, here.' He waved at me and I unsteadily made my way to his side.

He grabbed the man by his hair a forcing his head back.

'You started this now, finish him,' he looked at me directly. Gone was the smile and youthful appearance as he pulled my dagger free from its sheath and placed it in my hand.

'No,' I said calmly, I do not deserve the honour he is yours

Guthrom.

'You decided in your wisdom to fight this man, you failed and, without my intervention, you would be dead. Have you learnt nothing?' He took my dagger and sliced it hard across the already blood-soaked throat, making sure the man had a good hold on his sword as he died.

Laying him gently on the earth, I heard him mention Odin's name as he walked away towards the others that gathered around my banner.

'Guthrom, why are you angry with me?' I shouted after him, not understanding his annoyance.

He turned on me, eyes staring with a look of contempt.

'You don't fight when you can't win. All that will do is bring you a quicker death. You continue to try to prove your worth that you are equal to all men, well you're not and never will be as long as you rush headlong into unwinnable battles. To be a warrior, fight smart and use what's between your ears. You're a woman, so you need to fight like one.'

Now was not the best time to argue. Guthrom was angry with me for sure, but it was born out of worry and love. I would have been dead had he not arrived in time. As I looked at the others, I noticed Cinead had arrived also and looked concerned as he approached me.

'You are injured. Let Manara take you back to Hundorp.' He said gently.

'No, it is nothing I will stay. I can still fight, I won't leave.' Erik smiled and pointed over my shoulder. I looked and was relieved to see Rognvaldr, Hakon, and Sigurd approaching.

There seemed to be a lull in the fighting. Many men were running away, climbing the sides of the valley, trying to escape the onslaught. We walked together towards the black mass that was still engaged in battle.

'Let's find Heggalund,' I snarled.

The pain had numbed slightly, but breathing was still an effort, as I blew blood from the nostrils of my broken nose. I winced as the bone cracked, using my sleeve to wipe away the weeping from my watering eyes. We were winning; I was sure of that. And as the rain ceased, a flash of lightning creased the darkened sky. I waited, listening, knowing it would come. I had dreamed this moment for so long and as Thors' hammer struck, I finally saw my mother's killer.

CHAPTER THIRTY-ONE

Heggalund stood surrounded by three to four hundred of his men. The battle had become fragmented, with pockets of combat threaded throughout the valley. There was no sign of my father, but I knew he was here, somewhere. What I could see was Eystein, leading his warriors directly at Heggalund and his men. It was a brave attack, as they outnumbered him, but he had fire in his eyes and his men screamed death as they surged forward.

'Let's join them. They need the help,' I bellowed. We had gathered around a hundred swords about us, and as we had weaved our way through small skirmishes, my eyes stayed fixed upon my nemesis. We kept killing as we moved, striking fast and without mercy. Movement seemed to help my injuries. My sword arm flourished with fresh kills and I could still use my shield for defence when needed.

Our arrival helped as we joined Eystein in the shield wall. He was relieved to see us and screamed in delight when he saw his two sons.

'The sons of Hundorp are here,' he screamed. 'For Odin, Your King and your people.' His battle cry had the desired effect and with a surge of renewed belief and loyalty, they broke the enemy wall.

I did not need an invitation and dashed quickly through the gap. The rest followed and before I knew it was less than twenty paces from my Heggalund.

He saw me and ordered several of his men to follow him. He marched straight towards me.

'Leave him to me Helga, get behind me.' Guthrom was pushing me back, hoping I would obey. Cinead, too, grabbed at my arm, but I was having none of it, breaking away from them both to reach him first. I was denied as one of his men turned on me, lashing at me with a short-handled axe. I blocked the blow, but the vibration sent a lightning bolt of pain through my side. I winced and staggered, but stayed upright. Planting my feet on the sodden ground, I waited for the next attack. This time I was ready and as the axe swung, I raised my shield to meet it. It stuck firm and as he tried to break it free, I pushed into him, forcing him to stumble. His death was swift as Erik finished him for me, his sword blade entering his chest. He almost split him in two, spilling his guts and spraying us both in warm, sticky blood. There was no time to reflect. Erik was already fending off another attack as I again looked for my mother's killer.

It was mayhem. There were so many people fighting, and many were dead or dying all around me. But there, in the middle of it all, stood the person I was looking for. His tattooed face grinned as he fought his opponent. I was so intent on keeping him in view that I did not notice who he was engaged with, but as I moved forward, I saw Cinead striking at him with all his might. Once more I was attacked, I shielded the blow and dispatched one more soul to Valhalla. It took little effort as my

assailant ran himself onto my sword in a frenzied and

uncontrolled attack. It was a distraction, no more, but I

screamed in anguish as I saw Heggalund stab his blade into

Cinead's midriff. I rushed him, overcome with despair and

anger. He sensed my approach and, pulling his sword from my

friend, met my attack head on. I slammed into him, attempting

to knock him off balance, but he was like a rock and it was I

who staggered backwards.

'I will kill you, you bastard.' I was about to rush at him again

when I remembered Cinead. I quickly glanced at him and could

see he was still alive. He was crawling through mud and so

much blood, I just preyed to Thor that it was not all his. There

was no time to help him as Heggalund attacked me.

His power and strength were immense as he lunged. Time

and time again, his blows forced me backwards, as I desperately

tried to fend him off. I was no match for him and with each

blow my will wilted that little more. He laughed at me and stood, opening his arms wide in an invitation to strike. I took the bait and as I pounced; he chastised me like a small child, hitting me hard with his shield boss. I fell hard and was disorientated, the world spun and I was at his mercy.

He could have killed me there and then, but chose not to, allowing me to gather my senses and rise again. He was enjoying himself, taunting me, urging me to attack him, beckoning me forward. It was then I remembered what Guthrom had said, *'fight smart, you're a woman, so fight like one,'* and so I did. I ran at Heggalund like a woman possessed. He raised his shield and readied his sword, resting it on the rim, waiting for my attack. However, this time I used a woman's cunning, I was a few paces off him when I dropped to my knees, my speed and momentum allowed me to slide across the slippery ground and with my shield in front of me I took his legs. He had no time to react as he fell over me onto his face. He was quick to turn, but I was faster, plunging my sword into his chest. It was not a killing blow, as in my haste, I had missed his black heart. He screamed out in agony, so I removed my weapon and struck again, this time at his throat. Again, I cursed my aim, as I only sliced it open a little. I jumped on his torso pinning him down, he had no strength left to push me off and I knew then he was mine.

The battle had ceased, and we were victorious, but I was unaware of this. As Heggalund spat globules of blood from his gaping mouth, I placed the sharpened edge of my sword against his neck and smiled.

'My name was Eithne, but now I'm Helga, daughter of Harald Harfagre. You murdered my mother and now I take my revenge.'

I was crying as I sawed into the bulging neck of the man I had hated for so long. He gasped and grabbed for his sword, but someone kicked it away. I looked up, I saw it was Guthrom, and I cried even harder. With every stroke of my sword, my hatred melted away. For once, I did not feel anger or uncontrolled. I felt only sadness and grief.

It was symbolic to remove his head, just as he had done with my mother. My sword could not sever it, so I stopped and searched for the implement that would. The axe was heavy, and it took all my strength to raise it above my head, but raise it I did, and for all those I had lost on this journey, I brought it swiftly down.

CHAPTER THIRTY-TWO

I ran to Cinead, who was lying on his back, staring at the clearing sky. Manara shook her head as I approached.

The sun crept out and cast my shadow across his face.

'Eithne, is that you?' Tears streamed down my face as he spoke my old name once more. I lay down beside him and placed my head on his chest, as I had done many times as a child. I sobbed as he placed his hand upon my hair.

'Don't weep for me, Helga,' he whispered, reverting to my Norse name. 'I will soon be with Odin. Maybe I will find someone else to torment me in the afterlife as I found you here in the living.'

'Don't go Cinead, please don't leave me here.' I felt bereft with grief. Cinead had been with me since I left my island home. He had nurtured me, guided me in the Norse way, taught me the language, and helped me survive in this foreign land.

'Heggalund?' he gasped, his voice weak and rattling.

'I killed him, Cinead, like I said I would, but the cost is too high. I can't bear to lose you.' He patted my head like a frightened puppy.

'You will never lose me. Wherever you go I will be there, always.'

Groa was right; the Gods are fickle. I had avenged my mother, my plan had worked, and we had been victorious. Yet in return for their favour, they had taken my greatest friend. I wanted to curse them like I did all those years ago when I was a child, but Cinead would not approve and neither would Groa; and as a reminder of this, Gunnolf appeared high on a plateau above the battlefield. Sensing my grief, he raised his head and howled; the sound reverberating throughout Gaulardal. Cinead was gone.

Father was elated to see me; he grabbed me tightly, pulling me close. I sobbed in his arms as Guthrom told him about Cinead.

'We will take him home, Helga,' was all he said, and I nodded in agreement.

I felt strange, detached from reality. I had spent seven summers dreaming of this day and now it was here I felt empty, lost. The familiar feelings of hate and loathing were all gone. All that remained was sadness.

As always, Erik knew just what to say to drag me back to life.

'When we get home Helga, let's get drunk, that's what Cinead would do.' He smiled, but I could see his sadness was as equal to mine, and that strangely brought me comfort.

As I looked around the battlefield, the scene staggered me. The rain had cleared and the sun now shone radiantly through the hills and peaks of Gaulardal. The Valkyrie would be busy this day as hundreds of bodies littered the valley floor, and the crows were already flitting from corpse to corpse, pecking and ripping at the dead flesh that stretched out before them.

'Odin will need a bigger hall after today,' said Guthrom as he brought Thunder to me. My horse kicked his feet as if glad to see me. Erik helped me up, and I yelped as my ribs reminded me of my mismatched duels.

The battle was over, and people were leaving. Hakon shook my father's hand and shouted a goodbye to Guthrom and myself. I waved, and he returned the gesture with a warm smile.

'Well, I guess this is goodbye, at least for now,' Eystein was grinning, pleased with the victory, no doubt probably more pleased that his Kingdom was still his. He had allied himself to my father, which was probably wise. His sons accompanied him. They looked exhausted and Rognvaldr looked so much older than his years and bore a deep laceration above his left eye. He saw my concern and silently mouthed that he was fine.

'I have forgiven you, Helga,' said a boyish Sigurd.

'For what?' I asked, knowing full well what he was referring to. He laughed before reaching up and grabbing my hand. He kissed it gently and bowed mockingly.

"Till the next time, Moon Maiden.'

As he left, Rognvaldr came close.

'Will I see you again, Helga?' he asked politely.

'I might visit if I have the time, we will see.'

'Maybe I should come to Vestfold. Bring Hella when she has recovered.'

'Yes, do that. I would like that.'

I bent down, wincing at the effort, but I could not leave without kissing him.

'I love you Helga, stay safe.' He embraced Guthrom and the others and then left without another word.

I watched him go as the others mounted their horses and made ready to leave. Manara as always shared Cloud with Erik.

We left the valley together, my father leading the way. We had lost many men, but we were still almost a thousand strong.

Suddenly, a small horse appeared by my side.

'You owe me,' said Finnulf.

'I know,' I admitted.

'I risked everything for you and we succeeded. You really owe me.'

'All right, I'm in your debt. What do you want?'

'I want a proper horse. This one is embarrassing, and a fine sword and shield, mail too, and a helmet. Oh, and I want to be part of your war-band, you owe me that much.'

I did not answer, as my thoughts had drifted elsewhere. I thought of home, not Vestfold, but my Island by the sea with its long sandy beaches and its circle of stones. I remembered my parents, as they were, happy and loving. I could almost smell the sea and the mackerel cooking on our open fire. I missed it all so much. But these were memories of a child, and I was no longer that child. I was a woman who had fought with, and against men. I was a warrior, a shield maiden. I still had much to learn, but this was just the beginning and only the Gods know what happens to me next and they, as we know, can be fickle.

THE END

Book 2. (Excerpt)

The story continues.

'The Journey to Dyflin.'

I struggled with Cinaed's loss, but I wasn't alone, many had lost people in Gaulardal.

My father designated a new piece of land that overlooked the town and river as a burial place. It was close to where Erik and I were attacked; the place where this had all began.

I blamed myself for Cinead's demise; my selfishness had cost him his life, and at times I was overcome with grief. It was strange, as the outpouring for my friend was in complete contrast to the emotions I had felt after my mother's death. I felt guilty about that and struggled to comprehend the reasons.

Asa tried to comfort me; explaining that I was just a child when my mother had been murdered. The barbarity of her death had struck me numb, and so I could not express my grief at that time. Instead, I had consoled myself with the need to seek justice and revenge, burying the turmoil deep within myself. But now Cinead was gone, I had released the chains that bound my heart, and that is why I felt so bereft. I cried not just for Cinead, but for my mother as well.

It took a while to prepare the land, and during this time, each mourned the loss of their loved ones. They cremated some on funeral pyres, their ashes collected and kept in containers until we could bury them with the others. The rest were dressed and prepared for burial.

I had helped Asa to prepare Cinead, combing his hair and beard as I wanted him to look his best for when he arrived in Valhalla. Asa left us alone. I held his icy hand and whispered, so only he could hear.

'Cinead, I miss you so much and want you to come back to me. What will I do without out you by my side? Who will guide me now? Keep me safe? I wish I had never put us in harm's way, I can't bare it. Groa warned me and I took no notice and now you are gone. I cannot forgive myself. I'm drowning again, but you are not here to save me. Cinead, what should I do?'

'You must move on.' I hadn't noticed that Guthrom had entered the room and was unsure how much he had heard. 'The greatest honour you can give Cinead now, is to live your life the best way you can.'

'But he died because of me.' I sobbed.

'No, he didn't. He died in battle, fighting for a cause with someone he loved. There is no greater way for a warrior to die than that. Cinead adored you, Helga, and saw something in you that the rest of us could not. He believed in you and understood your ways. He told me you were born of magic, that you could see and hear the dead. When your mother spoke to you in the waves, he knew then that the Gods had plans for you. He loved you so much. So, grieve today, then live for him tomorrow.'

For all my sorrow, Guthrom's words did console me, and as the fading light painted mournful shadows across the landscape, I joined the others in my father's hall.

There have been many feasts and celebrations in Vestfold throughout the seasons, but this one was different. Many had died in battle before, but this seemed more significant. Something had changed, the winds had altered direction and my father was drunk.

'Helga,' he spluttered. 'Come here, daughter.' I shook my head, but he was adamant. He waved his hand, beckoning me; and someone pushed me forward. I turned to see Erik standing with Manara and he gestured for me to join my father, who had now climbed upon a bench so all could see and hear him.

He placed his hands on my shoulders to steady himself and kissed the top of my head affectionately.

'People of Vestfold, we have won a great battle, but the cost has been high. Valhalla is overflowing and more places must be found at Odin and Freyja's tables to accommodate our brave warriors.'

People banged their drinking horns in agreement, and several cheered. My father raised his hand and silence descended.

'I see faces here that I love, men and woman that have supported me in my quest to unite our lands. You have built my boats, fixed my sails, and stood with me in the shield wall. You are all my family.' Everyone listened intently to my father's words. The revelry had ceased and a respectful hush filled the hall.

'Some faces are missing now, and although I know they are content fighting amongst themselves and drinking with the Gods, their loss leaves a mark on us all. Every death hurts me; but one in particular touches my family the most.' He looked at me and I knew he was talking about Cinead.

'Cinead was a lovable man, gentle, caring, yet a fierce warrior in battle. Like Helga, he was not from these shores, yet in many ways, he was more Norse than I am, and I can now say the same of my daughter. So it is for this reason that I have decided that Cinead will have a burial fit for his status. He will be laid in one of my boats and buried with the others on the hillside. So if they tire of Odin's hospitality, they can always climb aboard and go Viking. I will make sure it is well stocked with chicken and ale.' Everyone laughed, knowing that Cinead was rarely seen without one or the other, or both.

'To Cinead… Skal.' The room erupted and tears streamed down my face once more. My father had given my friend the greatest tribute, and as his arms encircled me, I felt him shaking with emotion and sorrow.

'Tomorrow, after the burials, come and find me, I have something for you,' he whispered.

We filled the rest of the night with eating, drinking, and singing. Stories were told, and we remembered those who had died. We laughed and cried and shared our grief, and as the daylight approached, our burden was lighter.

I fell asleep, draped across Asa's knee. I was emotionally drained, and it was not long before I drifted off into a world of dreams…

'Eithne,' the voice was faint, but my name was clear.

'Cinead, is that you?' I asked.

Darkness surrounded me, yet something or someone stirred before me.

'It is.' I looked again but could not see him and in frustration, I called out.

'I can't see you where are you?'

'I'm in Dyflin.'

I awoke with a jolt, and Asa grabbed me.

'Helga you're fine you were just dreaming.' She exclaimed, trying to make herself heard above the feasting.

'Cinead, he spoke to me,' I yelled.

'It was just a dream.' She assured me, but I was not so sure.

'I need to find Guthrom. Where is he?'

'He left a while back and will be fast asleep by now, I imagine. Leave him be, you can speak to him tomorrow.'

It was a glorious morning; the sun seemed to shine brighter than it had ever done before, and it hung proudly in an almost cloudless sky.

They had used horses to pull the boat up the hillside, and now I watched as men gently lowered it into its ultimate resting place. It was partially buried, and only the deck remained above the ground. I watched as they carefully placed Cinead on board, laying his shield across his chest and placing his battle-axe in his right hand. Chickens were sacrificed and placed at his feet and a barrel of ale accompanied them, as my father had promised.

Friends positioned other items around him so that he would not forget them on his journey into the afterlife.

My heart ached as I stepped forward and crossed from the world of the living into the realm of the dead, if only for a short time. I knelt beside Cinead and watched as a breeze picked up a strand of his hair and draped it over his closed eyes. Nuzzling it to one side, I kissed his forehead, as he had done to me several times over the passing seasons. I reached down and removed my knife from its pouch and tucked it into his belt. Next, I took off the necklace that Asa had given me as a child and placed it in his left hand. I was a woman now, and no longer needed it for comfort. Finally, Manara handed me the Wolf banner that Guthrom had made for me.

'Keep that with you, Cinead, so I can find you in the afterlife,' I whispered.

I didn't want to leave him; I just sat there wanting him to open his eyes and hug me as he always did, lifting me skyward and crushing my battered ribs. There was nothing left for me to grasp on to, no hatred and no revenge. Cinead was dead, struck down by the same man that killed my mother. Heggalund had taken two precious people from me, and although I had killed him for it, his death brought me no comfort.

'Helga, come with me, let him be.' Erik reached out and took my hand and together we stepped back across the threshold. I walked away and could not look back as they buried Cinead under a mound of dirt. Over the next few days, we buried many more alongside him, each with stones laid around them to resemble the shape of a boat. Cinead had a fleet of ships and they could all sail to Valhalla together.

Later that afternoon, I looked for my father and found him alone in his chambers. He looked tired, and I wasn't convinced it was just the over indulgence of ale that caused his weariness.

'Father, you look unwell, you should get some rest.' I suggested.

'Yes maybe so, it has been a trying few days, but first to business.' His terminology surprised me, it was not the usual way he would address me.

'There is no simple way to do this, so I'm just going to say it,' he said awkwardly. 'Cinead has left everything he owned to you.'

For a moment I was lost for words, then I smiled, for I knew that he had very little regarding wealth, or so I thought.

'He has? I don't quite know what to say, father.'

'I can see by your reaction that, like me, you believe that Cinead lacked wealth or cherished goods; but our friend had a few surprising things stashed away from our years of trading and raiding, and now they are all yours.'

I was now intrigued, and wondered what he had left me. My father reached down by the side of his seat and produced an item wrapped in a blanket that had seen better days. He handed it to me and I unwrapped it gently.

The sword was stunning. This was no ordinary sword, and not one I had ever seen in Cinead's hand.

'It's beautiful. Where did it come from?' I asked.

'He told me he got it from a King who owed him a lot of coin because of a gambling debt. It is a rare blade.'

'It is Father, what is this inscription?'

'+Vlfberh+t it means Bright Wolf, rather apt don't you think? Cinead believed it held magical powers and wanted you to have it upon his death.' I stroked the blade and felt its power, its strength. This was no ordinary blade, this was a sword made for the Gods.

'Follow me, there is more.' My father led me through the busy streets of our town until we reached a small dwelling that overlooked the river. It was a beautiful spot, within walking distance of our town, but far enough away to enjoy the peace and tranquillity of nature. I could feel Cinead's presence here.

'This too is now yours,' my father said.

'How come I never knew of this place? He never brought me here.'

'It is sometimes nice to have somewhere for yourself, to get away from the madness of our world. Life takes its toll, and we all need a place to recover from our wounds and torment. Cinead would come here from time to time. It was his haven. He liked to watch the boats and would fish the river. Sometimes he would ask me to join him and we would talk and drink ale into the early morning. We usually talked about you.'

'Me?' I enquired.

'Yes, he told me I would never tame your spirit, that I must let you determine your own destiny. I once asked him why you were so difficult, so rebellious. He said it was because you had Pictish blood and flaming red hair.'

I found that amusing. Cinead knew me so well.

'I saw you at Gaulardal during the battle. Just for a moment, I glimpsed the same spirit and fearlessness that I saw in your mother all those seasons ago. Your skills are raw, Helga, but your passion is larger than the mountains that surround us.

Your people are warriors, just like mine, and I know I can never

curtail your fighting spirit. Yet there is more to you than just

that. You are cunning, devious and manipulative. You love and

hate with the same intensity. Men and woman will die for you

and you for them. In time, you could be an outstanding leader,

maybe even a Queen, if you survive that long. I have spoken

with Guthrom. He and Erik will continue to train you to fight,

since that is what you have always wanted, however there is

one condition.'

'What is that, father?' I asked warily.

'You will marry to secure an alliance. I have discussed it with

Asa and we think it will bring significant benefit to our region

and secure the peace for a while at least.'

'What!' I gasped, stunned by the proposal. 'I will not marry,

father. How can I live out my destiny if I am tied by such

womanly strings, I will not do it, not even for you.' I stood

angrily and began pacing back and forward. 'How could you

even suggest such a thing?'

'I thought you would be pleased. Rognvaldr seems a suitable match, and it's not like you don't know him. According to Guthrom, you have spent quite some time with him. He's of high status and Eystein thinks he's just what you need, a calming influence. I could marry you to someone else if you prefer, perhaps one of the more mature Jarls from Danmork.' He smirked, knowing that I loved Rognvaldr. However, I had not considered marriage.

'If I agree to this coupling father, I too want something in return.' He raised his eyebrows, surprised by my bargaining.

'And what would that be?'

∞

I spent the night alone in Cinead's home and after father left; I sat on a small wooden bench outside and watched the sunset fall into the river. It streaked the clouds with red and purple splashes and, as the sun extinguished, I wept once more. With the death of Heggalund, there was little more for me to achieve and I felt more alone now than ever before, or at least that is how I perceived it.

Everywhere I looked I saw my friend, and my grief was overwhelming, his bed was covered in furs, a few of them looked old and well used. I was certain they were the ones they had wrapped us in on my journey here all those moons ago. I undressed and climbed under them. I could smell his scent, and my sadness enveloped me. Alone and exhausted, I wished Rognvaldr were here to comfort me, to cradle me in his powerful arms and tell me that everything would be all right.

Father had posted a few guards to keep watch over me, an unnecessary act, but one that made him feel more at ease. I reached out and stroked Bright Wolf; running my fingers down its sharpened edges before grabbing the hilt in my hand. I would always keep it close, just in case. I had a reputation now and my enemies may consider seeking revenge for those I had killed, just like I had done. I wondered if any of those I had despatched were fathers whose children now saw me as a monster and wanted me dead. I had never considered that before; that maybe one day someone might seek me out to deliver his or her revenge. To end my life. Let them try, I thought, let them try.

Sleep took me swiftly, and just for a change I did not enter the world of dreams. I slept late and was woken by voices outside my new dwelling. I quickly dressed and strolled over to the door. Lifting the wooden bar from its resting place, I pushed it open and found Erik and Manara sitting together on the bench I had sat upon the night before.

'Thanks for waking me up,' I sneered. 'What do you want?'

'Well, that's a friendly welcome,' said Erik. 'We thought you might like some company.'

'Are you ok Helga?' Manara enquired, showing genuine concern.

'Yes, I'm fine,' I lied, but I knew she could see right through my facade and as her arms encircled my body, she whispered.

'I am always here for you.'

Just then Guthrom and Finnulf arrived, carrying a pot with left over stew from the night before, some bread and a selection of fruit.

'I thought you might be hungry,' Guthrom suggested.

Although I had feigned annoyance, I was pleased they had come and appreciated their company. We sat and ate together, reminiscing and reliving the events that had brought us to this point. It was not the same without Cinead, and I knew that my friends missed him as much as I did.

'How are your ribs?' Guthrom enquired.

'Still tender, but I'm eager to start my training again.'

'There is plenty of time for that. I hear you are to be married soon?' Guthrom announced.

'When did this happen?' asked Erik, his eyes wide with

surprise. 'Who would be so stupid enough to marry you?'

I blushed, and he knew instantly.

'Rognvaldr… Well, well. I never thought you were the marrying type, Helga.'

'It was father's idea, not mine,' I complained. 'He wants to secure the alliance with Eystein.'

'You still owe me a horse, Helga,' Finnulf moaned.

'You will get your horse, and all the other things you wanted, Finnulf. You will need them where we're going.' The others stopped eating and looked at me.

'Where are we going?' asked Manara.

'Dyflin.' I answered and Guthrom smiled. 'We're going to find Svanhild and bring her home.'

'How are we going to get there? Swim?' Finnulf enquired.

'I have a ship, a wedding present from our King. All I need is a crew, and I think I can persuade my future husband to help with that.'

Laughter is a great healer and our camaraderie brought us even closer together, but we all knew that Dyflin would hold many dangers and the chances of us finding Guthrom's daughter were slim, to say the least. But I had made a promise, and I intended to keep it.

Winter would soon arrive and I would spend it honing my skills and preparing my ship for our journey. When the ice melted and the trees budded, we would climb aboard, row the river, then leave these shores and sail westward. Cinead was waiting for us.

Authors notes

Although this tale is purely a work of fiction, there are certain people, places and events that are real, as far as I can ascertain from my research.

The trouble with Viking history, is that it is often fragmented, with little, if any, real early historical documentation. Names often overlap and inconsistences are rife, making it a nightmare at times to ascertain who is who, and what, and when, events actually happened. Since my story is based around Norway 860's AD, I had to explore many online resources and books to pick out certain events and information that would help me weave a plot around the history.

As many of you will know Harald Harfagre (Finehair) was a real person and did unite many petty kingdoms, becoming in theory the first King of Norway. He does have links to Vestfold, which he inherited from father, Halfdan the Black, and did have a wife named Asa Hakonsdottir, whose father was indeed Hakon Grjotgarthsson. However, Åseda, the wife of Eystein Glumra (Iversson) and the mother of Rognvaldr and Sigurd, had no real family connection to Asa or Hakon. They were all real people, but the connection is purely fictional.

As for Guthrom, he was also real. Full name Guthorm Sigurdson he was the brother of Harald's mother Ragnhild, however his daughter Svanhild and his injuries, at the hands of Kvist and Oddar (fictional characters) is all on me.

Helga (Eithne), is of course, a product of my imagination, as is Erik, Finnulf, Cinead and Manara. Groa however, can be found in Norse mythology. A volva (seeress) and practitioner of seiðr, she is mentioned in the Prose Edda written by Snorri Sturluson, most notably in the story of Svipdagr.

She was also known as the Goddess of Knowledge.

Both Hundorp and Gaulardal valley are both real places in Norway, and according to Heimskringla or The Chronicles of the Kings of Norway by Snorri Sturlason; a battle did take place in Gaulardal. It is said that Earl Hakon Grjotgardson came to King Harald from Yrjar and brought a great crowd of men to his service. Harold then went into Gaulardal and had a great battle slaying two kings and conquering their dominions.

I used this to form the foundations of my final battle, where Helga faces Heggalund. Obviously, I took a few liberties, as all writers do, but I hope I captured the essence of the time period and the hardships and brutality these people sometimes had to face.

For all this is a brutal historical tale of murder and revenge. I hope after reading it you find the real story held within its pages. One of love, compassion and family. After all, we are all stronger together, and it's only when we are divided that the shield wall breaks.

As for Helga, her story is just beginning and I hope you will join me and follow her into the next instalment of her life.

Her journey to Dyflin.

Milton Keynes UK
Ingram Content Group UK Ltd.
UKHW012334040324
438864UK00003B/4/J

.